8/12

MURDER AT
THE BLUE OWL

MURDER AT THE BLUE OWL

□   □

LEE MARTIN

ST. MARTIN'S PRESS
NEW YORK

Every person, place, and event in this story is totally fictitious. Any resemblance to any real person, place, or event is totally coincidental.

Design by Judith Stagnitto

Library of Congress Cataloging-in-Publication Data

Martin, Lee, 1943–
    Murder at the Blue Owl.

    I. Title.
PS3563.A7249M87   1988   813'.54   88-1846
ISBN 0-312-01795-2

First Edition

10 9 8 7 6 5 4 3 2 1

For T
Who made a Useful Suggestion

MURDER AT
THE BLUE OWL

□ PROLOGUE □

THE LAST OF THE credits trailed across the narrow screen in faded black and white, which to my mind was preferable to the pathetically garish early attempts at color of the other film. I hoped it would be a very long time before I had to sit through another Margali Bowman double feature, but of course I couldn't say so when the great lady herself—now plain Marjorie Lang of Fort Worth, Texas—was my hostess.

The lights came up and we all began to stand and stretch. All, that is, except Margali, and I could barely restrain a chuckle when I saw that Margali herself had dozed off. Although that shouldn't have been too much of a surprise, given the quantity of liquid refreshment Margali had imbibed during the course of a very long day.

Fara—my friend Fara Johnson, who had been responsible for the waste of my weekend with this debacle of a party—leaned over her, which was a feat in itself. The Blue Owl, a sixties-style counterculture movie theater, crams about 200 seats into a basement room not much larger than my living room, and getting in and out of the seats is not easy. Fara looked vaguely disgusted as she touched Margali's shoulder. "Mother!" she said. "Mother, wake up!" She stood back, bewildered. "Sam?"

she said uncertainly, looking toward her stepfather rather than her frowning husband.

Sam Lang said briskly, "Marjorie! Wake—" He grabbed her jeweled hand and then abruptly let go.

I should have guessed then, when he suddenly looked completely blank, when he turned helplessly to me and said, "Deb—"

I should have guessed, but I didn't, not until I touched her hand myself, a limp, cold, flaccid hand not yet beginning to stiffen but definitely no longer capable of voluntary motion.

And it would be convenient, even restful, to be able to call this a natural death. But I'd brushed past the back of her seat as I went to touch her, and when I stepped into the light, there was blood on the sleeve of my blouse.

Who would be most likely to follow instructions exactly? I looked around. "Harry," I said to my husband, "get everybody out into the lobby and keep them there." To my new son-in-law I added, "Olead, call 911. Tell them you're calling for Detective Debra Ralston. Give them the location and say we need a medical examiner and—" I hesitated. But friends or not, it had to be said. "And a homicide unit."

Turning to look again at Margali—or Marjorie, as nobody but Sam had called her in at least fifty years—I hoped I was through being morning sick.

□ 1 □

Not that it was morning now. In fact, as I gloomily considered the few possible suspects and waited for the onslaught of officialdom—and reporters, in the unlikely event that Margali had been telling the truth—morning felt about six months past. I remembered Margali at the breakfast table, no more than fifteen hours earlier by real time.

"And they're going to film it *here*!" she'd squealed, in affectation of girlish excitement, bouncing in her chair so eagerly that the pink peignoir that would have looked luscious on her twenty or thirty years ago fell into a less than enchanting—at least to my possibly jaundiced eyes—state of dishabille.

Her assembled houseguests, routed out for breakfast at what I considered an obscene hour on a Saturday morning (especially after a Friday evening spent watching videotapes of faded black and white Margali Bowman movies) and herded into an oppressively dark and formal dining room complete with Jacobean sideboard, Irish-linen tablecloth, and overlarge chandelier, regarded her with more or less—depending on the person—apparent pleasure at her revelation.

A slight young Mexican woman nobody had bothered to introduce to me padded silently in with a large blenderful of a frothy orange-juice mixture, set it on the sideboard, and plugged it in. "Serve breakfast now?" she asked.

"Oh, let's wait a moment, shall we?" Margali asked sweetly. "Edward, dear, would you say a blessing for us?"

I'd eaten at Margali's table many times before, always without the formality—which was surely all it was, for her—of a blessing. But that was before Fara belatedly found a spouse.

Edward-dear, Fara's husband, had come to the table in a navy blue plaid shirt, long-sleeved, with a clerical collar that did not quite conceal his extremely protuberant Adam's apple. Without replying directly to Margali's request, he bowed his head for an impromptu five minutes of haranguing the Almighty on subjects having nothing to do with the food, after which he pronounced a loud and solemn "Amen!" that was echoed almost inaudibly by Fara. "You may serve now," Margali told the servant, who vanished as silently as she had come.

Margali reached for the blender on the sideboard and turned it on for a brief whir before pouring a generously full glass of what looked to me like a rather fuzzy semifrozen orange juice. "None for me," Fara said, eyeing the concoction with unconcealed distaste.

Margali looked around the table and then, beaming, presented the glass to Harry. Approximately two seconds later, I heard him choke. "It's half vodka," he whispered to me.

He didn't need to have said it. In my—as my mother would put it—delicate condition, the smell had made itself unpleasantly obvious. Margali was offering me a glass now, beaming with owlish delight as the overfilled tumbler puddled onto the gleaming tablecloth, and I managed to say, "No, thank you, I'm sure it's delicious but it's—uh—much too early in the day for me."

"We never indulge in alcoholic beverages," Edward pronounced, in a voice that sounded as if it should be booming from the pulpit in an old-fashioned tent revival. The comment may not have been needed. Margali hadn't offered it to him, and now the Mexican girl—she looked about seventeen, and I wondered about her green card—was bringing him a glass of milk.

Jimmy Messick, Margali's only (so far as I know) son, rescued the dripping glass. "That's enough, Mother," he said. "If any of the others want any, they can serve themselves. Maria," he added sharply, "*traiganos jugo de naranjas sin—sin* addition.*"

"Your Spanish is execrable," Sam Lang remarked, apparently to his plate, "and her name is Lupe."

"I call them all Maria," Jimmy replied. "Anyway, she understood me."

She must have; she brought in a large pitcher of what was this time apparently plain orange juice, and as I gratefully sipped at it, Margali served herself from the blender and tossed off half the glass, faster than I can drink an Orange Julius, before returning to her announcement. "I don't guess anybody understood me," she said pathetically, with an expression I believe is referred to as making a moue. "I don't mean it's just going to be filmed in Texas; I mean right here in Weatherford, right here on the ranch! So I don't have to leave my darling, darling family!"

Her speech was peppered with audible exclamation points, and Jimmy drawled, "Mother, you're caricaturing yourself." Margali looked at him reproachfully before returning to the orange-juice concoction.

The Mexican servant—Lupe—slid a breakfast plate in front of me, and I looked down at altogether too much of everything, everything being scrambled eggs, buckwheat cakes, hash browns, and sausage links. Turning hastily away from the overabundance, I noticed Fara, fifteen or so years older than her half brother, staring at her plate and poking nervously with her fork at a sausage link that appeared to have been drenched with maple syrup.

I couldn't imagine why Fara had invited me to this party; we'd grown more and more apart over the years. Was it because of Margali's new show? But Fara had seemed uninterested in the show, whether or not it was news to her, and she'd scarcely said ten words to me since hurrying in late last night, well after the video event had begun.

Sam was gazing at Margali, his eyes unreadable. He wasn't excited, either. Nobody in her family really seemed interested in her announcement. Puzzling. If someone was going to film a big new television series—something planned to rival "Dallas" and "Falcon Crest"—at my house, I'd be delirious. But of course Fara and Jimmy hadn't grown up here; this ranch was Margali's baby. As best as I had been able to determine, Sam had bought it four years ago at her urging, after she decided that as the home of some really big stars Weatherford had a certain cachet she ought to cultivate.

I didn't see why. To me it was just another small town on the uncivilized side of Texas.

But there was another factor I reminded myself to take into account. Fara and Jimmy had grown up with glamour—too much of it. Margali had been a star well before I ever began to notice movies; I remembered how horribly embarrassed Fara had been when the other girls at school learned who her parents were. She was living, fairly contentedly, with her grandmother—Margali's mother—in Fort Worth, and walking to grade school the way we all did. But the summer between our fifth- and sixth-grade years, Fara was gone two months, and that fall one of our classmates showed up at school with a fanzine. There, in living color, was a photograph of Fara herself, captioned "Margali's Mystery Child Revealed!" There were photos of Fara with Margali, and insets of all Margali's husbands past and present, including, of course, the late Prince Ali Hassan, Fara's father.

Of course we teased, and of course Fara cried. Then, for some reason, I became sorry for her, because even at the age of eleven I could sense that despite all the glamour, despite all the money, Fara was lacking something very important that most of the rest of us had. So I went out of my way to treat her as a casual friend, neither to lionize nor to sneer at. And in return Fara clung to me as if I were her only lifeline to a sane, real world.

That was the reason Fara had followed me all the rest of the way through school; that was the reason I'd made several long visits to Hollywood in the days when it *was* Hollywood; that was the reason I'd gotten letters and telephone calls from Fara through the years, even if the intervals between them had increased; and that, I supposed, must be the reason Fara had seen to it I was invited to Margali's birthday party.

But why this one, I went on wondering. Margali had a birthday every year. I'd never been asked before. Maybe this was a special one—her age, of course, was discreetly omitted from the invitation, nor would anyone be rude enough to ask.

Sam was still staring at Margali, but his expression had subtly altered, and I thought, with no realization then of the instant detour in my train of thought, Why, he doesn't even like her! He doesn't like her at all. I wonder—

But I wasn't sure what I wondered. Sam, I recalled, had been Margali's first husband; I wasn't sure how many others had intervened before she and Sam were married the second time, this time in a marriage that had lasted—I couldn't recall how long.

"Deb, do you feel all right?" Harry's worried voice cut into my reverie, and I realized I had been swaying slightly, staring intently at Sam, for longer than I meant to. I shook myself slightly and looked back dismally at my overfilled plate, hearing Margali chattering on and on about the wonderful new television series—I had managed to miss its name—and its wonderful producer and its wonderful sponsors and all the wonderful, exciting things that were going to happen in it.

None of the ideas sounded very wonderful and exciting, or even original, to me, and it occurred to me that her family's blasé reaction need not be due, as I had guessed, to the fact that they were used to the glamour. Because—was there really going to be a television series at all? Or was it something Margali had cooked up in that fertile imagination of hers and convinced herself was true?

Now, with no apparent transition (was I falling asleep at the breakfast table?), I found myself staring at Margali. She'd been discussing her role for a minute or two now; it sounded rather a Joan Collins-type character. Well, Joan Collins, no matter what her age might happen to be, is a truly beautiful woman. But Margali? I knew theatrical makeup artists could work wonders, but Margali? Now?

"Debra, you haven't touched your breakfast!" I jumped as Margali's voice, now in an affectionately chiding tone, was for a moment directed at me. And of course she called me Debra rather than Deb; Fara, in desperation, had dragged me along on several lengthy visits with her mother when we were teenagers. Margali had greatly enjoyed the maternal role provided it didn't last too long (I often wondered whom Jimmy had been farmed out with), and I remembered her proudly—and rather awkwardly—preparing us breakfast with her own fair hands, leaving an incredible array of dirty dishes and pans in the kitchen for the cook to deal with later.

If I was Debra then, of course I was Debra now; never mind that "then" was thirty years ago, and the awkward shy teenager was now a veteran police officer whom no one ever called Debra.

Margali couldn't let all that be thirty years ago. Because if it was thirty years ago, and Fara and I were the same age, then Margali would have to admit that she was old enough to have a daughter in her forties. And if she had a daughter past forty, then she herself would have to be at least in her sixties, and though even that was probably well below her real age, it was a lot older than she'd ever admit to.

I didn't even bother to wonder how she was maneuvering her subconscious around the fact that my grown daughter Becky was sitting at the table beside her husband Olead Baker, who was the close friend of Margali's grown change-of-life baby Jimmy. I was fairly certain that Margali had not yet figured out that Becky was my daughter.

I was also fairly certain Margali had no intention of figuring that out. What you don't figure out, you don't have to know.

She was still looking reproachfully at my filled plate.

"It's delicious, but really, I'm just not very hungry right now," I muttered.

"But Debra dear—"

Harry leapt nobly into the breach. "She really doesn't ever eat much breakfast, Margali," he said.

Margali. Not Mrs. Lang, or even Miss Bowman. Just Margali. Never mind that he had just met her the night before, and that she was at least half again his age. Of course everyone was calling her Margali. "It makes me feel so old when anyone calls me Mrs. Lang," she had told him, laughing deprecatingly.

But you are old, Margali, I thought, and I wish you'd realize it. I don't believe there really is going to be a television show at all. I haven't seen you in twenty years or more, not in real life, not in a movie, not on television, not even on a silly little quiz show or talk show. You are old. You're older than Joan Collins. You're older than Liz Taylor. You were past playing the ingenue before either of them ever thought about walking across a stage or a screen. And both of them wear their age well. You don't. You are old, Margali.

And then I was instantly ashamed of myself. That seemed vicious, and I didn't feel vicious. I just felt sorry—sorry for Margali, caught in her own web of self-deceit, sorry for her family, who had to live with this obscene mockery and—some of them at least—mourn it.

Fara did, anyway. Fara loved her mother; of that I was sure, and I couldn't imagine why she would want me to see Margali as she was now, so unlike the Margali I'd loved so many years ago.

Perhaps that was when I really began to wonder why I'd been invited. I'd thought about it before, but not hard; now I was thinking hard. It wasn't really likely to be friendship; Fara and I weren't even that close, not anymore; we'd gone in such incredibly different directions, I thought, glancing again at Fara and Edward Johnson.

Apparently their church, whatever it was—I'd never quite figured out—eschewed not only alcohol, coffee, tea, and tobacco, in which they agree with several more orthodox churches, including the one I had begun sporadically attending, but also short sleeves, haircuts for women, stockings that weren't opaque, skirts shorter than halfway between ankle and knee, and makeup. Looking at Fara, I wondered whether they also had an objection to soap and water; her once blue-black hair, now streaked with gray as mine was, was coiled into a greasy-looking bun, and her sallow face didn't look quite clean.

Her two daughters crouched over their breakfast plates scooping up hotcakes and maple syrup and richly glazed sausage links and gulping fresh orange juice as fast as their pale little mouths could open. The eggs were ignored; apparently they were no treat. Both girls, seven-year-old Esther and five-year-old Dorcas, were wearing identical high-necked white blouses with sleeves buttoned at the wrists, limp dark cotton skirts with uneven hems that brushed their ankles, and black Mary Janes; their hair, like Fara's, was gathered in buns that looked too heavy for their little necks.

Impulsively I asked, "Edward, what is the name of your church?"

"The Evangelical Full Gospel Church of the Risen Redeemer," he said precisely, and bit off his words.

Involuntarily I said, "What?"

I shouldn't have. He repeated it. Every word, just the same.
And he didn't say anything else.

I have been at crime scenes friendlier than that breakfast
table. Sam Lang, an oilman wealthy and influential enough not
to have been saddled with the tag of "Margali's husband" even
at the time of their first marriage, sat morosely and stared alternately at his plate, at his stepdaughter and her husband, at his
stepson (with a little more affection; I couldn't imagine why),
and at the blender, which the maid kept unobtrusively refilling.
Except for the one comment to Jimmy, he said, so far as I can
remember, nothing at all the entire duration of the meal.

Jimmy Messick ate. And ate. And ate. Lupe didn't try to refill
his plate; she just kept replacing emptied plates with full ones.
He must have been tremendously well supplied with nervous
energy, because he was quite slim despite his incredible ap-
petite. But I had a hunch I knew where the nervous energy
came from. He twitched; his fingers twitched; his eyes
twitched; and his mouth twitched; he reminded me of Roddy
McDowell playing Caligula (had he ever? If he hadn't, he
should have). I knew Jimmy and Olead had been roommates,
off and on, when both were able to have roommates, at Fort
Worth's most expensive and exclusive private psychiatric hospital, the Braun Clinic. Olead was completely over whatever it
was (undiagnosed now because the young Dr. Braun didn't like
diagnoses) that had sent him there. But looking at Jimmy's
hands, his mouth, his watery eyes, I wouldn't have wanted to
bet that Jimmy was.

On the other hand, I'd have been happy to bet that a thor-
ough search of his room might be extremely enlightening.

Fara ate timidly, glanced timidly at her mother, glanced timidly at her husband, glanced timidly at her timid daughters, and

went on eating, every little bite precisely cut and squared on the fork.

Edward Johnson, of the clerical collar, fed himself rather mechanically, staring into a great distance as I suppose befitted someone who apparently thought he had not only direct, but also exclusive, access to the Almighty. He spoke only once more, to order the girls to eat their eggs. They hastily obeyed, Dorcas, the younger, stuffing a forkful of eggs into a mouth already full of hotcakes and nearly choking herself. But under that stern regard, she managed to control the coughing until, aided by milk, she succeeded in swallowing the horrendous mouthful. Edward resumed staring into the air.

That was the family. The rest of the house party, all but one, was unexceptional. The guests included Bob Campbell, a sandy-haired middle-aged man who'd been introduced to me as Margali's attorney; Carl Hendricks, a very ordinary-looking balding man in his mid-sixties who'd been introduced to me as Sam's business partner; and Darlene Cooney, a briskly cheerful woman apparently in her thirties who seemed to be Margali's personal secretary or companion.

The last member of the party puzzled me distinctly. It wasn't that I didn't know her. I did, rather well. But she didn't seem to be a particularly close friend of anybody in the family, and it wasn't her habit to follow her patients around.

I wondered who—Margali, Sam, Fara, Jimmy—had seen fit to invite, to this weekend house party to celebrate Margali's birthday and her (alleged) new show, Dr. Susan Braun, one of the finest psychiatrists in Texas.

What kind of birthday party couldn't go on without a police detective and a psychiatrist on the guest list?

Susan was, I suppose, dressed more appropriately for a weekend house party at a Weatherford ranch than any of the rest of us. Not that the ranch was actually in Weatherford, a little town of only a few thousand people about twenty miles west of Fort

Worth. But the telephone lines came out of Weatherford; the mail was addressed to Weatherford; and the public services, what few there were, came either from Weatherford itself or from elsewhere in Parker County.

Susan was wearing cowboy boots (that wasn't unusual; I couldn't recall ever seeing her out of cowboy boots), a beige divided skirt, and a blue chambray work shirt gaudily embroidered with multicolored parrots. For her, this was everyday attire.

She didn't look like a psychiatrist.

She is often told that.

I am often told I don't look like a cop.

I didn't that day, either. I was wearing black polyester slacks with a rather loose waistband and a shirt that had been in style several years ago under the name of "big shirt." A "big shirt" is intended to look seventeen sizes too big. It is intended to be worn with a cinch belt by those whose waists are small enough (that means about sixteen inches), and with a gaudy sash by the unfortunate others.

I, of course, was one of the unfortunate others. I hadn't gotten up the nerve yet to tell my captain of my two-and-a-half-month pregnancy, and I wasn't about to announce it to Margali Bowman before telling my captain.

Margali's voice faltered to silence—even she had to realize at last that she was talking into a vacuum—and suddenly I pitied her. I leaned forward in my best I'm-paying-attention manner and said, "I'm sorry, Margali, my mind went to wandering. I guess I'm not quite awake yet. What was it you were saying?"

Margali looked vague and turned again to reach for the blender. Darlene forestalled her. "Now, Margali, it's time for our vitamin, isn't it?"

"It's time for mine. I don't know about yours," Margali said distinctly. She stood up and swept from the table, gathering the flowing skirts of her peignoir around her with a gesture I was pretty sure she had copied from Loretta Young, who does it much more gracefully. Darlene followed her out, leaving me wondering whether she was a companion or a nurse.

Jimmy stood up too, laughed, and snatched an apple from the overfilled fruit bowl in the middle of the overly large table, sending a cascade of oranges rolling onto the floor. "You're going riding, aren't you, Olead?" he asked into the silence, as Fara, intercepting a majestic glance from her husband, bent to collect the oranges.

"Riding?" Olead sounded pleased.

"Yeah. We always ride when we come out to the ranch for the weekend. The horses'll be saddled and up by the patio waiting by now, even the Shetlands for the kids." He looked, without much affection, at his nieces.

Dorcas gazed imploringly at her father. Esther, not quite as timid, whispered, "May we be excused to go riding?"

Edward stood, nodded to the girls, and strode out, with the girls and Fara pattering after him.

Olead, still very much the newlywed, glanced at Becky, who was looking as eager as he was. He had the money to buy two or three stables of horses, but as a busy medical student, what he didn't have was time to ride. Nor did Becky, who was in the process of becoming adoptive mother to Olead's three-year-old half brother.

"Harry, why don't you go on and go?" I heard myself saying, as Margali slipped back into the room. "I really need to get a little more rest."

"You're not riding?" Susan demanded, stopping abruptly and staring at me. She rode nearly every day; she'd declared that the mentally ill need recreation and exercise even more than the rest of us, and her clinic included a riding stable in addition to jogging tracks, a gymnasium, and an indoor swimming pool. I'd ridden with her some during the summer.

"I really don't think so, Susan," I said as feebly as I could manage. "I'm so terribly overtired."

Susan didn't answer; she gave a quick look at Margali's departing back before turning to follow the others. Then she stopped, turned around, and looked at me again. "Maybe it's better if you don't ride now, since you're not really very used to it."

I sat with my mouth open. I hadn't told her a thing.

But of course a psychiatrist is, first of all, a medical doctor.

I strolled out onto the patio to watch the others mount up. I love horses and riding; any other day I'd have been out there too. But not now; I didn't dare. A first pregnancy at forty-two is nothing to play games with.

And this was my first. My other three children were adopted; I'd long since dismissed from my mind even the barest possibility of pregnancy. Until the end of September, when my doctor carefully explained to me the real meaning of what I'd taken for a combination of beginning menopause and a flare-up of an old ulcer.

I still wasn't sure I believed it. But I was taking no chances.

I stood and watched.

Margali also had wandered out onto the patio and from it to the lawn, still in the increasingly bedraggled pink peignoir with orange juice and vodka spilled down the front of it and maple syrup on the sleeves. She was meandering, not quite steadily, around in the milling group, patting horses' noses; some of the horses, not liking her breath, shied away from her. "Darlene, you really ought to go," she said in her most saccharine voice. "Especially since dear Debra has decided to stay with me. You can take her horse."

That wasn't exactly what I'd said I was going to do, and Darlene's no-nonsense face looked doubtful.

"Ah, come on, Darlene," Jimmy said boisterously, as his horse, matching his own mood, pranced and circled. "If we stand here much longer waiting for you to make up your mind, the horses'll shit all over the roses."

"Jimmy, your language!" Margali squealed. "Why, dear Debra will think you have no manners!"

"She's heard worse." Jimmy grinned insolently at me.

"You might as well come on, Darlene," Sam said. "The horse is already saddled, and Marjorie's just going to have a little rest now, aren't you, Marjorie?"

For a moment the two stared at each other and then Margali replied, in a barely audible voice, "Yes, Sam, I was just going right now. Have a nice ride." She turned and scurried toward the house, lifting the hem of the peignoir so that I could see fluffy pink slippers matted with dew, and blue-veined ankles that were bony rather than slender.

"Come on, Darlene," Fara urged in her barely audible voice, glancing at Edward as she always did when she spoke. "It would be nice to have another woman along, since Deb's not going."

"That's no reason," Jimmy objected. "You've got two other women already."

"Another one besides," Fara said. "I mean, we're sort of out-numbered."

Edward, who to my surprise had mounted easily, harrumped at that, but Darlene was finally persuaded. With her astride the horse that had been intended for me, the riding party headed toward the lake, leaving behind rose bushes that had been, as Jimmy warned, rather liberally bespattered as well as, in a couple of spots, chewed.

Thankfully, I turned toward the bedroom that had been as-signed the night before to Harry and me. Turned, and almost ran into Margali, who was standing just inside the patio door staring after the departing riders.

"I thought they would never leave," she said breathlessly. "I want to show you something, Debra, but it's a secret and you have to promise never, never to tell!"

"I promise," I agreed warily, backing away from the vodka

fumes that were threatening to reawaken my only barely ended morning sickness.

"It's a secret. They're trying to kill me for it, Debra, and you'll know what . . ." The rest of her sentence trailed off into incoherence, and she turned and dashed through the door, leaving me to wonder whether I was supposed to follow her down the hall.

□ 2 □

BY THE TIME I could reopen the door that Margali had slammed in my face and get into the hall, Margali was completely out of sight. I stood for a moment just inside the closed door, wondering why I was so tired, and then went on into the—whatever you call it. Living room, I guess, but it looked more like a hotel lobby. There were six couches grouped strategically around little tables too small to hold anything useful, and the rest of the floor was dotted here and there with chairs, potted palms, and an occasional artfully arranged floor cushion. The brick fireplace—the modernistic style with no mantel—seemed carefully planned to emit no heat whatever, and through the triple-size sliding glass doors I could see a wooden deck with a sloping lawn behind it.

The whole room was somehow unreal. I was sitting in a movie set. Cary Grant, circa 1939. Any minute now the beautiful spy with red hair and a Swedish accent—Margali Bowman as Greta Garbo—would tumble through the sliding glass doors pursued by the sinister Japanese or German. And then Cary Grant, with a debonair smile and a shiny black .45 automatic, would step from behind a potted palm.

Margali never acted with Cary Grant. She wasn't that big a

star. But in her own mind her importance grew in direct proportion to the length of time it had been since she'd made a movie.

I rubbed my eyes and looked again for some vestige of comfort, of homeliness. There wasn't any there for me to see.

The room contained no television (that was in the den, a monstrous big-screen abomination), no books, no magazines—I could imagine no possible use for it at all except, maybe, cocktail parties. And this would be an idiotic place to hold a cocktail party, when all the guests presumably would be driving from Fort Worth and would have to drive back to it after several drinks. Why not just hold the party in the town house in Fort Worth to start with? The town house that is a famous landmark mansion in Ridglea?

I told myself I was being catty. She might have a lot of house parties like the one I was attending at this very moment, full of guests who came and stayed for days and weeks, the way they do in English novels.

I went on being catty. Who, I wondered, having been to one of Margali's house parties, would ever want to go to another one?

But that hadn't always been true. I could remember over thirty years my girlhood joy whenever an invitation from Margali came.

Yes, I was older now. There was a lot of change in me. But unless my memory was completely gone, there'd been a lot more change in Margali. And it might have been very recent, for all I knew.

When I got a chance to talk with Susan—but I didn't know when that would be. The ride was likely to be a long one.

There was still no sign of Margali. I could be alone in the house, except for the hum of a vacuum cleaner in one of the distant bedrooms and an occasional clatter from the kitchen. "Margali?" I called.

She didn't answer.

Resignedly, I sat down. At least there was one useful thing in this—whatever this room called itself. A telephone, sitting on a spindly little white and gilt desk, a telephone that—Margali had announced to all and sundry last night—was on a metro line, so we could call just about anybody we needed to call.

I didn't want to think about what that was costing her. A metro line provides local calling privileges all over metro Dallas, metro Fort Worth, and the Mid-cities, all the way east to Plano. If you live on the west edge of Dallas, or the east edge of Fort Worth, or in the Mid-cities, you can get one for not much over the cost of a regular local line. But if you live in any other exchange, you pay extra for every quarter of a mile to the closest Mid-cities exchange. We found that out when we lived—temporarily—over in the Camp Bowie area and tried to get a metro line. I don't remember how much it would have cost us. All I remember is that we didn't get one.

It was at least another twenty miles from that apartment to this ranch house. Maybe more.

Unless there was someone here who *lived* on the telephone— and she seemed fresh out of teenagers, and one thing I did know was that Sam did all his business out of Fort Worth—it would be far cheaper just to pay the toll charges.

On the other hand, it was possible there was somebody—like maybe Jimmy—who'd just as soon not have a record of his calls to Dallas and Fort Worth.

I was being nosy again. Reminding myself I wasn't on duty, I picked up the phone and dialed my own number.

With fear and trembling, I'd left Hal at home alone this weekend. He was old enough, he'd insisted, not to need a baby-sitter.

He's old enough, Harry had assured me. Now quit worrying.

He should be old enough. He's sixteen now. And I'd asked the neighbors on both sides and across the street in front and across the alley in back to look out for him. It wasn't as if we'd abandoned him. But all that didn't mean I wasn't worrying.

After all, it wasn't two full months ago that somebody tried to shotgun him.

All right, tried to shotgun me. But Hal was in the car.

He answered me on the third ring, with an unconcerned "Hi, Mom!" that grated on my nerves. Didn't he know how worried I was?

"How'd you know it was me?"

"Had to be. Because Vickie already called and Grannie already called and Sammie's out riding. I told him I couldn't go," Hal assured me with an air of great virtue, "because my mom and dad are gone and I have to look after things at home."

"I hope you're not telling everybody we're not there!"

"Just Sammie. Well, and a few others."

"What did Vickie say?" I asked resignedly. If word hadn't already reached every burglar in the Summerfields area that Harry and I were out of town, it never would.

"She said she was in Oklahoma." Hal paused. "Or maybe it was Ohio."

"You sure it wasn't Oregon?"

"Yeah, well, maybe it was Oregon."

"Hal, look at a map," I said. "If your sister left Fort Worth on Friday afternoon to go to Tulsa, what would she be doing in Ohio or Oregon on Saturday morning? Anyway, Tulsa is in Oklahoma."

"Oh. What'd she have to go to Tulsa for anyway?"

"She didn't have to, she wanted to."

"Then why'd she want to?"

"To visit Don's parents."

"Why'd she want to—"

"Hal," I said, "go clean up your room."

"How do you know—"

"Your room always needs to be cleaned up."

To a resounding chorus of "Oh, *Mom*," I hung up and shook my head. My older daughter Vickie has been married several years now to an attorney named Donald Ross Howell III, and with that name he'd just about have to be an attorney. But unfortunately their bankroll isn't as impressive as Don's name, and they're still paying off school loans—a lot of them. This would be only the second time Don's parents had seen five-month-old Barry.

Hal has lived in Fort Worth all his life except the first three months, which was how long it took us to get him from Korea to Fort Worth and get the adoption process moving. How in the world could he not know Tulsa is in Oklahoma?

Ohio? Oregon?

And had Margali gone to Ohio or Oregon? Whatever it was she wanted to show me was taking long enough.

"Margali?" I called again.

This time she answered me, from the wing of the house that contained the family bedrooms. "In a minute!"

I continued to sit and look around me. The room's arrangement wasn't as haphazard as I'd thought at first; there was some frail amount of order in the planning, and although no two of the couches or chairs exactly matched each other, they all tied together in a fairly harmonious pattern. It would have been quite an attractive hotel lobby. It was just that I couldn't imagine why anybody would want to live in it.

But actually, nobody really did, except the housekeeper, whose own suite of rooms was a little apartment. Margali used it for weekend house parties; Sam brought business guests here for deer hunting, or quail hunting, or fishing, depending on the time of the year. Maybe Jimmy used it, but I'd hate to guess for what.

I wondered whether Fara and Edward-dear used it. It'd be a decent place for religious retreats, I supposed, except he'd want to hide the bars and the—well, maybe it wouldn't work so well for the Evangelical Church of the—whatever it was he said, I thought, finding my eyes fixed on an awfully interesting wall hanging. Nice bright silks. Interesting colors. Really interesting colors.

And I abruptly abandoned my attempt to persuade myself to notice only the colors. *This* wasn't Cary Grant circa 1939; more like Linda Lovelace circa 1972. Where in the world did Margali get a thing like that? As prissy as she was, she couldn't possibly have ever really *looked* at it.

A thump at one end of the room attracted my attention. Margali was back; she'd tripped over something—or nothing—but caught herself. At least the peignoir was gone; she was now wearing magenta slacks, white spike-heeled sandals, and a yellow blouse that clashed unbelievably with her badly dyed red hair.

She had to be lying. Nobody could possibly have offered her a glamour role—at least not unless they did it sight unseen.

Her heavily jeweled fingers, the nails two inches long and bright with magenta nail polish, were clutching a brown envelope, which was overwrapped with a plastic bag of some kind. Clutching it to her breast, she looked around furtively. There was nobody for her to see except me; the monotonous hum in the bedroom cut off briefly and then resumed, and the occasional clatter in the kitchen went on. That was all.

"We need to go out onto the patio," she said. "That way nobody will hear."

"Margali, it's going to rain," I objected.

"Not yet. Not quite yet. And you never know who's listening—they've suborned the servants, even—"

"They've done *what*?" Telling myself I ought to be a dutiful guest, I disentangled myself from a chair that had felt far more comfortable than it looked and followed her back down the long dark hall that led through the guest-bedroom area and out onto the patio.

The sky in the northwest was a deep blue-black now, although in the east it was still blue and the morning sun was shining. This wasn't just a storm coming in; this was the first blue norther of the season. And the Texas blue norther is an incredible phenomenon. It's called a "blue" norther because the frigid weather from the northwest gives an eerie blue-gray look to the approaching storm system; we say there's nothing between West Texas and Alaska but three bob-wire fences and two of them are usually down. Well, that's not true, of course, but the Rockies form a natural trough, and the winds that sweep down their eastern walls ricochet off and pour south and east. One time I remember visiting relatives, standing on a patio south of Amarillo looking at an outdoor thermometer, waiting for a blue norther to strike and watching the mercury drop. It was going down so fast I could see the movement.

That's part of what a blue norther does. And if the northbound weather coming up from the Gulf is wet and warm, the collision between the two produces incredible thunderstorms that spawn tornadoes. That was what we had coming this time. I could see tongues of lightning licking at the clouds, that was how close to the storm we were, and yet close to the ranch house the air was so still, so dead, I was suffocating in it. The kind of time when you sit in the detective bureau and tell war stories until everybody gets tired of war stories, and then you sit there in silence until after a while some old-time officer says, "What we need now is a good homicide to clear the air."

Usually we get one, when the air's like this.

I did not want a good homicide to clear the air. I didn't feel like a cop at all right now; I felt like a woman who wanted her husband to come and comfort her. "I wish they'd get on back with those horses," I worried, sheltering my bare forearms with my hands and feeling the fine hairs standing on end.

"They will," Margali said, a throwaway line. "Look, Debra, dear, I need to show you—"

I turned. With great care, she had stripped off the plastic bag from the brown envelope and was holding the bag under her arm so that the wind wouldn't whip it away. She opened the brown envelope, and now I could see that the thick bundle of papers she lifted out formed some kind of legal document: It was legal length, covered with that thick blue cover lawyers use.

"What is it?" I asked.

She recoiled and looked sharply at me.

"If you don't want to tell me, that's okay," I assured her.

"Well . . ." She continued to stare at me. "Promise you won't tell?"

"I promise." It was an easy promise to make. I had been a police officer long enough to recognize insanity. I was looking at it now, and wondering why I hadn't spotted it last night or earlier this morning. That was something Susan could handle. So whatever Margali wanted to tell me, I wouldn't need to repeat it.

And I was glad I wouldn't. It's different when you're on duty, when you're dealing—usually—with strangers. But I'd come here as a guest, not as a police officer. I wasn't working a case. I was just being Debra. And I felt oddly embarrassed, uneasy, at receiving unwanted confidences from a woman I remembered as funny, charming, no more odd than a milkman's daughter would expect a movie star to be.

Margali sat down abruptly at one of the tables that dotted the patio. "They're trying to kill me," she said breathlessly.

My pitying mood instantly vanished. That was a line from one of the movies we'd seen last night, and she'd even recaptured and reproduced the same delivery. But I reminded myself that even hypochondriacs can get sick; even paranoiacs can have real enemies. "Who is, Margali?" I asked, seating myself across from her in a white mesh stacking chair.

"I don't know. Some of them. But I don't know which ones."

"You want to tell me about it?" That question, of course, I had to ask, not just as a cop but as a human being.

"I'm trying to. Only I don't know what to say."

I made encouraging noises, and Margali took a deep breath. "I got sick last week," she told me.

"Yeah?"

"I mean I was really, really sick. Really, really sick." Her voice trailed off, as if she had forgotten what she was saying, and she sat quite still, only her hands moving slightly, nervously, on the surface of the table. Dingy diamonds failed to cover the huge brown age spots, the protruding blue veins, on those hands that now picked at the stapled top of the sheaf of papers.

I thought suddenly of a Japanese movie I'd seen last year, about an old warlord who decided to divide his territory among his three sons. His voice had trailed off like this, as he sat at conference.

He'd gone to sleep, abruptly, in the middle of a state picnic that followed a boar hunt, and all the vassal lords sat and waited for him to waken. But only one son tried to protect him from the noonday sun.

He had a jester who hopped like a rabbit. The jester loved the warlord but hated what he'd become.

Was I becoming Margali's jester?

She sat staring vacantly at the scudding clouds. After a moment I prompted, softly, "You were really sick."

She jumped. "Yes. I mean I was—well, my stomach was all upset and it was just burning and burning and burning and my hands and feet felt tingly and funny, all funny, you know—"

"That sounds pretty miserable," I agreed, sitting as still as she was.

"It was awful! And, and, that's arsenic poisoning; I know because I did a movie one time. I was this lady and she was getting poisoned by her husband, only she found out what was happening and—"

"Well, but—"

Suddenly, now, she was wide awake again, bouncing in her chair as she almost shouted across the table.

"And so I had to, you know, learn about arsenic poisoning, so I'd know how to act, and they gave me this book about it, and it was an awful, awful book, only that's how I know—"

"But the thing is—"

She wasn't going to let me talk. I wasn't quite sure she even knew I was there, by then, except as part of the background scenery. She might be—probably was—sincere, but she couldn't stop acting even for this.

"And so Sam called the doctor and the doctor came out and then they got that other doctor, the one Sam invited here this weekend, that lady doctor—I just don't see how ladies could be doctors, do you, all that blood, but—"

"Well, actually, Susan is—"

"But anyhow, they both said I wasn't really sick at all, I mean I was just throwing up and throwing up and I felt so awful and that lady doctor took some—some *specimens* to test; you know what I mean, so nasty?" She shuddered, did not give me time to talk, and went right on. "And she came back and told me it wasn't arsenic at all and said if it was, she could have told, but I know she was lying and she's in on it and—"

She stopped and began scrabbling on the table, looking around wildly, and then she sprang to her feet and dashed over to a closed cupboard beside the barbecue grill. Opening it, she said over her shoulder, "I don't know what to do, because now they've got that awful Darlene woman and she just watches me and watches me—"

"Have you been sick anymore?" I asked, turning slightly to watch her now myself.

"No, but I know they're just waiting for everybody to forget— I would have called the police, but I knew they wouldn't believe me, not when that lady doctor said—"

"Margali," I interrupted, "I know Susan Braun."

"Who's Susan Braun?"

"That lady doctor. The one you're so worried about. I know her. Honestly, no matter what anybody else said or did—and I certainly don't know Sam or Jimmy that well—I can assure you that Susan is telling the truth. If she says she didn't find any arsenic, then—"

"How would she know?" Margali demanded, frantically moving bottles back and forth. I wondered what exactly she was looking for.

But that, at least, was an honest question and deserved an honest answer. "There are chemical tests. A lot of them, now, but the first is over a hundred years old."

"Really?" She turned briefly to stare at me before returning to her search through the cupboard. "But what if—what if you were *sick*? And you threw it all up before the doctor got there?"

"You wouldn't. Some of it would stay in your system. It'd get in your hair and fingernails, that kind of thing. Don't you remember reading about Napoleon?"

"Napoleon?" She sounded baffled. "I was going to be in a movie once about Napoleon. I was going to be Empress Josephine. Or maybe it was Empress Carlotta."

She sounded as vague as Hal. Oregon or Ohio. Empress Josephine or Empress Carlotta—a little difference between the two. Even I knew that. She could play Carlotta now—Carlotta, the deranged widow of a deposed and executed puppet monarch, living on and on in a court of dreams and shadows; maybe that was the only role she could play now.

But she shook herself, as I'd seen her do before, and walked over to set a Diet Coke in front of me. Sounding almost like the old Margali, she asked, "What about Napoleon?"

"Just, modern analysis of his hair, coupled with some really incredible detective work, has been able to prove not only that he was poisoned with arsenic, but even who probably did it." I opened the can. It tasted flat. I didn't know an unopened soft drink could get flat.

"Then that's why . . ." Her voice trailed off again, and she glanced uncertainly back at the cabinet.

"Why what?" I asked, wondering where I could dispose of the unwanted drink.

"Why that lady doctor wanted to cut my hair. I wouldn't let her. Maybe I should have let her."

"Maybe you should have," I agreed, not knowing what else to say. "But you said she took samples—"

"She wouldn't let me *flush*," Margali said. She was staring at me now, and incredibly, at her age, an ugly mottled blush was stealing over her face.

"Oh, *that* kind of sample."

"I mean—I mean, after I threw up."

"I thought that was what you meant. She'd have been able to tell from that, really, Margali. So if she didn't find any traces of arsenic, there just weren't any to find."

"Then maybe it wasn't arsenic. Maybe it was strychnine." She was pawing through the cabinet again.

I managed not to laugh. "Margali, arsenic has about the same symptoms to start with as any other digestive upset. That's why it was so hard to diagnose until chemical tests for it were invented. But strychnine doesn't work that way. If you had taken strychnine, everybody around you would know it."

"Really?"

"Absolutely. I promise. The symptoms are pretty awful." One doctor I knew had inelegantly and not quite accurately described a strychnine victim as rolling around the room like a hoop snake. I wasn't going to say *that* to Margali. But if I had to, I'd tell her about the uncontrollable convulsions, the incredible arching of the back until the victim may be supported only by his head and his heels. Hoping she wouldn't ask, I hastily added, "As far as the vomiting and all . . ."

I paused, watching her. She didn't ask why. She'd found the whiskey, and she turned, with the bottle in her hand, to say, "That's a bad word. *Vomiting,* that's an ugly word. Can't you just say *throwing up?*"

I wondered how she'd have reacted if I'd said *puke.* But she was waiting for me to speak. I went on. "Throwing up can be caused by a lot of things. Just because you were throwing up doesn't mean you were poisoned. You could have had a twenty-four-hour virus, something like that—"

"I never, ever get sick," she objected.

"Or maybe you'd had a little too much to drink—"

"I *never* drink too much," Margali said indignantly, downing a shotglass of whiskey in one gulp and putting the bottle and the used glass back onto the shelf while continuing to clutch the bundle of papers under her arm.

"Okay." I didn't intend to argue. "It might have just been something you ate, then. But honestly, Margali, if Susan said it wasn't arsenic, then it wasn't arsenic, and it couldn't possibly have been strychnine."

"Well, they're still trying to kill me." She looked around wildly. The plastic bag had slipped out from under her arm. "Catch that!"

I went chasing across the yard after it, but the increasing wind had caught it and it was gone. "Sorry," I said, returning to the patio, "but I guess you'll have to get a new bag."

"How?"

"There're bound to be some in the kitchen."

"In the kitchen? Why? That attorney gave me this one. Why would they be in the kitchen?"

"Take my word for it," I said. "Most people keep plastic bags in the kitchen."

"Oh," she said, looking down at the brown envelope. "Oh, well, I guess this'll do."

She turned, reopened the cabinet, and poured another shot of whiskey. She used a different glass this time.

I reminded myself the maids must be used to her. Most likely they came out every weekend after she had left and replenished this shelf with full bottles and clean glasses.

I still didn't know what it was she wanted to show me. She'd gotten sidetracked on *they*—whoever *they* might be; they wanted to kill her with nonexistent arsenic.

To the best of my knowledge, I've never seen a case of arsenic poisoning, and I've been a cop almost sixteen years. I wonder whether it's even still done anymore?

I guess if it is, they're still getting away with it. They always did, unless they did something incredibly stupid such as poison fourteen people from the same family, or let somebody see them soaking flypaper in the water they made the tea with. You just don't ever suspect it. Not unless you're a little paranoid to begin with.

Which, I suppose, means that if you're paranoid, you're probably not going to be poisoned, but if you're sane and somebody wants to poison you, you're fair game.

I was beginning to feel as paranoid as Margali.

This drink tasted horrible. I'd like some of that whiskey too, I thought, only I didn't dare have any. My doctor had warned me, quite sternly, about something called fetal alcohol syndrome. He said there are enough risks in a woman my age having a baby without adding to it.

So I just watched Margali drink. Juggling the bottle and glass, she reopened the empty brown envelope and looked in it. "Where—"

Her voice began to rise to a high wail, and I hastily interrupted. "The papers are under your arm. Don't you want me to carry something?"

"Oh, no, thank you, dear, that's very kind of you." She set the bottle and glass back on the table.

She was back to being the gracious lady. I wondered whether she knew Margali at all anymore; I wondered whether there even was a real Margali left, under the layers and layers of roles she had played over the years.

Finally she got to the legal document again. This time she went a little further. She actually handed it to me.

It was, as I had surmised, a will.

"That's why they want to kill me," she said.

"Because of the will?"

"Because of the will."

"Why?" I asked. "If they want money that badly, why don't you just *give* them some?" That was, I admit in retrospect, a very silly thing for me to say. But as much experience as any police officer gets in dealing with weird situations, I can still find myself with nothing whatever to say when it's my very own weird situation. Sort of like going straight to lunch after working a shotgun murder, and then turning green two days later because some little Cub Scout chucks his cookies at a pack meeting.

"Oh, it's not *that*," Margali said in a shocked voice. "They have plenty of money. But they want me to change my will."

"Margali," I said without thinking, "that doesn't make sense. If they want you to change your will, then why would they want to kill you? The only way you could possibly change it is if you're alive."

"That's why I won't change it!" she exclaimed triumphantly. Reaching out to pat my hand, she said, "Oh, Debra, dear, I *knew* you would understand. Nobody else does, but *you*—"

I knew exactly how Alice felt when she fell down the rabbit hole. "Margali, I think I'm lost. I mean, you said they want you to change your will, and you said they want to kill you, and if they want you to change your will, they've got to keep you alive, so why would they want to kill you?"

"I *knew* you would understand," she repeated, still leaning over to pat my hand with that jewel-bedecked painted claw.

"But I *don't* understand," I said loudly.

Unfortunately I was drowned out by a loud crack of thunder nearby. Margali jumped wildly—so did I, for that matter—and cried, "What was that? Is somebody shooting at me again?"

"Thunder. That storm is getting closer and closer." Indeed it was; the wind now was picking up summer's dust and whipping it into our faces, and I was more than ready to go in. But Margali seemed not to see the storm.

Then I realized what she had said. "Again? Did somebody shoot at you?"

"Last week. Only Sam said it was a car backfiring." She leaned back, looking and even sounding almost complacent. For some reason this didn't seem to bother her as much as the imaginary poison had.

"Margali," I said as carefully as possible, "maybe it *was* a car backfiring. You see, most murderers use the same method over and over. Poison and a gun call for two completely different kinds of personality. It's very unlikely that one person would—"

"But you just said there wasn't any poison!" she cried in shrill triumph. "We have to talk fast now—" She leaned over me, breathing whiskey fumes directly into my face.

I couldn't help it. I backed up.

A stunned expression leapt into her eyes, and I thought fast. "Margali, please do excuse me, but I think I'm coming down with a cold and I wouldn't want you to catch it. It might interfere with your television show, and that would be—"

"Oh, dear, yes, that would be dreadful, how very thoughtful of you!" Backing away from me, she became very businesslike. I wondered what role she was playing this time. It must be from one of her movies that I hadn't seen.

There were a lot of her movies that I hadn't seen. I didn't *want* to see them.

"All right. It all began six months ago." She stopped.

"What all began six months ago?"

"That was when I made this will."

"Who knows what the will says?" That would be a starting place, if indeed there were any basis to this farrago of nonsense she'd been telling me.

"Oh, nobody except that attorney, of course, it just wouldn't do at all for them to read it."

"What attorney? Bob Campbell?"

"Oh, no, not Bob, he might have told Sam. A different attorney. I forget his name. He was in the phone book."

"Margali, how could anybody be trying to get you to change your will if they don't know what's *in* your will?"

"Oh, they know what's *in* it, they just don't know what it *says*."

If I turned my head would chessmen be walking around the landscape? Would a large white rabbit run by looking at a pocket watch?

"Margali," I tried again, "who knows what's in it?"

She was leaning back, looking very pleased with herself, face alert with that quasi intelligence of the insane. "Oh, they all do."

"All who?" What would it take to penetrate her brain? Or was that even possible?

"All of them. Sam, and Fara, and Jimmy—all of them."

"Is it Sam and Fara and Jimmy you think are trying to kill you?"

"Oh, no!" She paused and looked very thoughtful. "Certainly not Fara. *She's* an evangelist!"

Evangelists have done awfully strange things before now. I did not say that to Margali. "Then who do you think it is? Sam? Jimmy?"

"Oh, I don't know! All right!" Looking agitated again, she had another quick slug of whiskey while I glanced surreptitiously at the will. It looked quite in order, at least so far as I could tell from the first paragraph or two.

"It all began six months ago. That's when I made the new will."

I did not remind her that she'd already said that.

"And then there was that awful wreck."

"*What* awful wreck?"

"I had a wreck. In my car."

I was surprised she hadn't had a dozen. "What happened?"

"It just wouldn't stop."

"Wouldn't stop?"

"Yes! And I'd just had the brakes worked on, so it couldn't have been the brakes."

"What was it, then?"

"Oh, it was the brakes." She poured more whiskey. By now I was nervously trying to remember just what blood-alcohol level it is that's fatal, and estimate what hers would be getting to by now.

"But you said—"

"It shouldn't have been the brakes, because they'd just been worked on, but Sam called the man and he said there was a little, little leak in some kind of hose seal and all the brake fluid fell out."

She didn't *sound* any worse than she had at breakfast. Maybe she went somewhere every now and then and reduced the alcohol content of her stomach. That wouldn't reduce her blood alcohol, but maybe it would keep it from rising quite so fast.

The brakes. "That happened to me once," I said. "It's really scary."

"But I had just had the brakes *fixed*."

"Did Sam take the car to the garage himself?" I admit I don't know much about the habits of millionaires. But I couldn't see one spending an unnecessary day waiting around at a brake shop.

"Oh, no, he sent Mike to do it."

Now maybe we were getting somewhere. "Who's Mike?"

"The chauffeur."

"The chauffeur," I repeated.

"Yes, dear, the chauffeur."

"Was Mike driving when the wreck happened?"

She looked startled. "Why, yes, of course, who else would have been driving? You don't think I drive *myself*? Oh, Debra, dear, I'm much too nervous to drive."

I could well believe it. "What did Mike say caused the accident?"

She leaned over me again. "He said the brakes failed. But of course he's in on it."

"Margali," I said, "*who* do you think is trying to kill you? And why?"

"Why, I told you, dear. They're trying to kill me because of the will."

I took a deep breath. Could I think of a way to end this discussion? "Well, I'll tell you what," I said. "I'll just keep my eyes open and if I see anything suspicious, I'll do something about it, all right?"

"But you mustn't *offend* anybody." She really meant that. Find out who was trying to kill her and why, but don't offend anybody in the process. The natural-born victim. She was damned lucky all this was just in her head, I thought to myself at that moment, because if anyone really *was* trying to kill her, he'd certainly succeed.

She was still watching me, eyes wide with apprehension. "I promise to be very careful not to offend anybody," I reassured her.

"I would feel ever so much safer if you would do that, then," she said. She glanced around and gave a slight scream. The horses were coming up the gravel bridle path at a medium gallop, and at the same time the rain started, not with a few mild sprinkles but with a sudden gush, as if someone had turned on fire hoses overhead.

· 3 ·

"THEY MUSTN'T SEE this—" Frantically Margali was trying to stuff the already-wet paper back into the brown envelope as the riders wheeled to head for the stable. "A special hiding place— I've gotta—"

"Margali, let's get inside." Her words didn't register. Not then. If they had, I might have suggested the inadvisability of hiding wills.

"They mustn't see—"

"They won't if we go *inside*!" I grabbed her hand and virtually dragged her indoors; the lightning and thunder were almost continual, and I expected the riding party was going to be stuck at the stable for a while.

She was still struggling vainly with the will, now wadded in an awkward bundle that she was attempting to force into the envelope. "Wouldn't you like me to help you?" I asked.

"Yes—please—you won't *tell*—"

"I promise not to tell." I refolded the will, tucked it into the envelope, and handed it to her, and she scurried off down the hall toward her own bedroom.

Turning, I sat down in a chair and thought, I certainly would like to get some sleep. My doctor had warned me I'd be drowsy all the time these first few months. But I hadn't known it would be like this.

And I'd rather work a double ax murder than try again to cope with a demented—friend.

It's easy, now, to look back and say I should have been able to tell something was really wrong. But I couldn't. Thing is, for every legitimate call any police department gets—any call where there's really a burglary, a robbery, a shooting, an actual police problem of any kind—there are probably ten false alarms. Not deliberate ones—those are something else again—just the kind where a concerned citizen *thought* there was something going on. The gun going off that was really a door slammed too hard. The prowler who's really the new neighbor who dropped his car keys. The kidnap in progress that's really a five-year-old howling because Mommy won't buy him Teddy Ruxpin.

You just don't ever know. Not for sure. You don't have any real way to tell who is, and who is not, mistaken; even if you could put every complainant on a polygraph, that wouldn't rule out the honest mistakes, or even the really good liars. There was the time all three members of a love triangle came into the police station at different times—on the same day—to report that the other two were conspiring to murder the one that was there telling the sad tale. We laughed about it, after they'd all finally gone. At least one of them was lying or nutty, we agreed. Probably all three. And Clint Barrington—he was my partner then; that was before he went over to the sheriff's office—drawled, "If we just sit here long enough, sooner or later every nut in Fort Worth will walk right straight through those doors."

Three weeks later the boyfriend shot the estranged husband in the back bedroom of the estranged wife's house. The boyfriend and wife insisted the husband had broken in and tried to kill them. There was substantial evidence, including our own tape recording of an hysterical telephone call to the police department, to support that claim. We had to let it go as self-defense. We had no choice, not with a court order commanding the husband to stay away from his wife, and a broken lock on the front door.

But I always wondered.

Because the wife was into voodoo.

And when I went into the house, there were four black candles on the mantelpiece, and a voodoo book lying on the bedroom floor with a bookmark placed at a spell: How to Lure Your Enemy to His Own Destruction.

The spell called for four black candles. I know because I read it, there in that dark bedroom, with the victim's brain tissue sprayed on the ceiling. Read it and thought, Well, if the four black candles don't do the trick, there's always the telephone.

So don't tell me that people don't get away with murder. They do it every day.

But all the same, I had no reason to assume there was murder—or even potential murder—here. After all, I'd known Margali, more or less, for over thirty years. She'd always been nervous; she'd always been high-strung. Now she was showing signs of alcoholism and of incipient, or actual, insanity. Sure, she'd made a complaint to me—an unofficial, unrecorded complaint—that somebody was trying to kill her. But the complaint made no sense whatever. Susan Braun was on the job. That was good enough for me. It was a psychiatric problem, not a police problem.

So I sat in that idiotic cocktail parlor of a living room, wrapped in the comfortably self-centered lethargy of early pregnancy, with my alert cop brain completely shut off, while maids vacuumed and polished and Margali fussed around in her bedroom and the rain pelted down outside, until finally the rain slowed to a trickle and the riders came up from the barn.

They came in through the triple sliding glass doors, all thirteen at once, and all completely drenched and shivering. Olead and Becky didn't stop; they headed straight for their bedroom.

Well, they'd been married only three weeks; I figured they'd have no trouble finding a way to warm up.

Sam hit the door yelling for Margali, and she came tearing out into the living room as if she expected to be whipped.

"I told you a year ago to get something done about the hot-water system up here!" Sam roared.

"I thought we might get a hot tub," Margali quavered.

"Hot tub's ass, we got one in town, that ought to be enough of that silliness. All we need up here is an extra hot-water heater. What the hell, first things first; Esther, Dorcas, hot baths now, hup, hup!"

Fara and Edward both stared at Sam as if he'd taken leave of his senses. "They'll wait their turn," Edward said.

"I say it *is* their turn," Sam retorted.

"They're my children—" Edward began.

"You run your house your way and I'll run my house my way," Sam shouted. "Those little things're chilled to the bone. Bath now, kiddies!"

"Take a bath *together*?" Dorcas demanded, wide-eyed.

"Thou shalt not look on thy sister's nakedness," Edward proclaimed.

Susan stared at him. "That's not in *my* Bible."

Edward glared at her for a moment and then decided to glare at Fara instead. "Come along now, children," Fara said softly, one hand on each child, marching them in the direction of the guest rooms. "One at a time, real fast, and then Daddy can get his bath."

Sam turned, muttering something under his breath, and stalked off toward his room, leaving the others standing in the living room dripping.

"Maria!" Jimmy bawled. "Hey, Maria!"

Lupe appeared so promptly she must have been waiting for his call.

"Get us all hot towels!"

"Hot towels?" Lupe stared at him.

"You know, towels? You get dry towels, you know, and you put 'em in the dryer and—"

Margali stood in the living room, swaying slightly as if totally bewildered by the chaos, and then headed purposefully toward the bar.

"Never mind, Lupe," Susan said, "there are plenty of towels in the bedrooms. I'm sure we'll all manage just fine." She and Darlene walked off together and Jimmy shrugged and took off too.

"No hot towels?" Lupe appealed to Margali.

Margali said something incoherent and wandered off. The lawyer and the businessman were gone too—I hadn't noticed them leave—and now the living room contained only Harry and Edward, who were staring at each other, and me. Edward turned and stalked off, and Harry said, "I've never seen such a mess in my life."

"What kind of a mess?" I asked.

"These *people*!" He gestured wildly. "This comic-opera ranch house! Ah, the hell with it!" He stalked off too.

I continued to sit in the chair. It seemed the best place for me, if all the bedrooms were full of wet people trying to get dry.

Susan came back in, a towel wrapped around her falling-down braids. "That Edward is the most incredibly nasty-minded little man I have ever seen," she commented to me without stopping in her trek toward the kitchen. She returned a moment later with a plastic bag she took toward the bedroom.

Lupe came out of the kitchen with a handful of plastic bags. "For wet clothes," she told me, and left them beside me.

It was the most practical suggestion I had heard all morning. I supposed it had originated with Susan.

After a while everybody got back into the—alleged—living room, and somehow it was decided—I'm still rather vague as to who decided it, because Sam was still too angry for coherence and Margali for obvious reasons was even more incoherent—that we would all leave here and go to the town house in Fort Worth. There was, after all, a heated pool there. An indoor heated pool. And a nice hot tub. And—

It sounded like a very good idea to me, especially when Margali added, as if by afterthought, that she'd ordered our lunch served there.

I wasn't quite sure how, unless I'd been asleep, but it had somehow gotten to be eleven o'clock, and I for one hadn't eaten much breakfast. I had very little hope that the atmosphere at lunch would be any better, but maybe at least it would be buffet style and we wouldn't all have to sit together.

And maybe at least I could ride back to Fort Worth with Harry and rejoice in a little bit of sanity.

No such luck. Margali decided I was riding with her. Nobody except Sam could successfully overrule Margali, I'd noticed, and Sam didn't seem to care who rode with Margali. Bob Campbell and Carl Hendricks were riding with him.

If we'd had our own car, we could have gotten away with arguing; I could have just said I was riding with Harry and that was that. But we'd left our car at Margali's town house and ridden out to Weatherford in Olead and Becky's van. So I seemed to be stuck.

"I think I'll just ride with you too," Susan said pensively. "Darlene, you don't mind driving my car, do you?"

Of course Darlene didn't mind. Margali did, but she had enough smarts left that she didn't want to argue with her psychiatrist even if she didn't think she needed one.

It would be pleasant to be able to say that it was an agreeable trip and everybody got along just peachy.

It would be pleasant to say that it was a productive trip, and we managed to get at the root of what was eating Margali.

In fact, the trip was neither agreeable nor productive.

I got carsick.

Picture this: a big gray limousine with a chauffeur, pulled over to the side of the road. The chauffeur sitting sedately behind the wheel with his cap pulled over his eyes. Margali in the backseat, driver's side, staring resolutely in the opposite direction. Dr. Susan Braun, in ranch pants and cowboy boots, topped with a brown corduroy jacket, out with me. And me, in slacks and big shirt topped with a blue nylon jacket six inches shorter than the shirt, off in the ditch barfing.

On top of that, Olead's brown Ford van, containing Harry, Becky, and, of course, Olead, pulled up behind us to see what is wrong.

I do not need a psychiatrist, a medical student, my younger daughter, and my husband to help me barf. I can do it quite well all by myself, thank you.

I managed to chase Harry, Becky, and Olead back to the van, although they wouldn't leave; the van sat there stolidly parked behind the limousine. But Susan wouldn't leave. She kept hovering around me, demanding to know what I'd had to eat or drink since breakfast. *"Nothing!"* I yelled at her between attacks of retching.

"Nothing nothing, or just nothing important?" Her eyes were full of worry, and as usual one braid was falling down.

"Nothing! All right, half a Diet Coke, but—"

"Was it from a can, or—"

I glared at her. "You sound as screwy as Margali—oh—" I was trying to say "oh, damn," but didn't manage to finish the second word for another minute or two. When I finally could talk again, I added, "Damn it, Susan, I'm *pregnant,* okay?"

"I thought so. Have you seen a doctor?"

"Of course I've seen a doctor!" She was hovering over me like a mama hen. *I'm* the mama hen. Olead called me that, last May, when we thought he was about to be executed for a murder somebody else committed. *I'm* the mama hen. I don't *need* a mama hen.

Susan did not care whether I needed a mama hen. "Have you been vomiting like that for long?"

"Yeah, for about five minutes." I was looking for something to wipe my face and hands on. Between Fort Worth and Weather-ford there's not even very much grass.

Susan started peeling Kleenexes out of one of those little purse packets and handing them to me a sheet at a time. "You know what I mean."

"Sometimes I get sick, okay? I mean, don't most people when they're pregnant?" All right, she was concerned about me, I shouldn't be that rude. I started over. "When I'm hungry, or overtired, or too hot; for instance, I can't wear anything on my head right now because if my head gets too hot—and I can't take my vitamins except after supper—"

"But it's nothing new?" she interrupted. "And the Diet Coke, was it—"

And suddenly I knew what she was getting at. I straightened and stared into a pale frightened face. "Susan, *was* there arse-nic when Margali—"

"No, no, of course not, I'd have been on the phone to you right away." Absently she began to pin up the straggling braid. Talking around a mouthful of bobby pins, she repeated, "No. But just about any heavy-metal poisoning would have the same symptoms. And I didn't test for anything else. Because—"

"Because it was Margali. I know. I wouldn't have either. All right. I drank half a can of Diet Coke. It was from a liquor cabinet on the patio. The can was sealed until I opened it. But—" I stopped, feeling like an utter idiot.

"But what?"

"You'll think *I'm* paranoid." And that was a stupid thing to say. Is being afraid of being thought paranoid a form of para-noia?

"You're not paranoid. But *what*, Deb?"

"It tasted flat. It—just tasted flat. That was why I didn't fin-ish it."

"What did you do with the rest of it?"

"Poured it out. Onto the ground by the patio."

Susan looked up at the clouds. At a conservative estimate, about five inches of water had dumped on us in the last two hours. *"Shit!"* she said, loudly and uncharacteristically.

"Susan, I really think the Diet Coke was okay. It had probably just been sitting out there in that liquor cabinet all summer, in that heat—I really think I just got carsick. I used to, when I was a kid. I feel okay now. And—"

"Yeah," Susan said. "But—keep me posted, Deb. If you start to feel sick again—especially if there's no apparent reason—"

"I will." I decided my hands and face were as clean as they were going to get without a bath. And Kleenex is biodegradable. I could leave the sodden mess on the roadside with a clear conscience.

But somehow I wasn't too surprised when Susan leaned over, picked it back up, and wrapped it neatly in the cellophane package she'd taken it out of.

We made the rest of the trip back to Fort Worth with me sitting in the front seat of the limousine beside Mike, who studiously avoided looking at me. I wanted to transfer to the van, but Olead pointed out—rightly, I suppose—that there was a lot of wind from the front that had just passed through, and the van was swaying like crazy. I would be much happier in the limousine, which is far heavier and has less wind resistance.

Maybe.

But it appears—unless Susan is right, and I really don't think she is—that I will be confined to riding in the front seat for the duration. I haven't gotten sick in the back of a car since I was seven years old.

So Margali and Susan were sitting in the backseat, as far apart as they could get (or at least as far as Margali could get from Susan), and studiously ignoring one another. Or at least, Margali was ignoring Susan. Susan, I think, was ignoring being ignored.

The ensuing silence gave me a little chance to think; apparently standing out in the cold rain barfing had wakened me a little, and I had at least temporarily shaken off the day's lethargy. I was thinking about Sam—Sam at the breakfast table—*Your Spanish is execrable*—like a college professor; and Sam after the ride—*hot tub's ass . . . what the hell . . .* Like LBJ, or at least like Sam Lang's impression of LBJ.

Which one was really Sam? Were they both? Was Sam as layered in contradictions as Margali was?

I wished I knew Sam better. As it was, I really couldn't judge, but two things I was sure of: Sam might still love Margali, but he didn't like her anymore, and Margali was afraid of Sam.

But there's a long way from an unpleasant marriage to murder. There are a lot more divorces than murders in this or any other state.

Behind me, Margali stirred. "So they poisoned you too," she said with gloomy relish.

"Nobody poisoned me, Margali," I said, hearing flat exhaustion in my voice. "I just got carsick, that's all. I'm sorry, I know I smell awful, but—"

She was leaning slightly forward, and it dawned on me that this car, like the patio, like the stage-set living room, like I supposed any place where Margali could be expected to spend any amount of time, had a bar. She was opening it. "Debra, could I get you something to drink?"

Debra. Not Debra-dear. Apparently getting carsick was déclassé; Margali wasn't nearly as fond of me as she usually was.

"Is there any Coke?" I asked.

There wasn't any Coke. There wasn't any 7-Up. There wasn't any Slice.

I settled for club soda and a dash of lime juice. The club soda was from a sealed bottle. The lime juice was not. I could tell Susan didn't approve, but I didn't care; I had to get that nasty taste out of my mouth, and there's no way enough arsenic or anything else that could do much damage could get into a dash of Rose's Lime Juice.

At least, I didn't think there was.

Susan asked the chauffeur whether he'd mind stopping for a moment right by T-Com so she could run in for a minute. She knew it was inconvenient, she told Margali, but it would save her an extra trip, and if nobody minded . . .

Nobody minded.

It wasn't, of course, to the Texas College of Osteopathic Medicine that she wanted to go, but to a small brick building right beside it, the small brick building that housed the Tarrant County Medical Examiner's Office.

There is a lot of testing equipment in that building. I've asked for the results from just about all of it, at one time or another. But it still felt very strange to know that the specimen that was being delivered now, stashed invisibly inside Susan's vast maw of a purse, came from me. Came from me, and was on its way to the toxicology laboratory.

We waited about five minutes before Susan came out, looking rather pleased with herself. "Well?" I asked.

"They'll let me know tomorrow," she said.

We hadn't gone into Sam and Margali's town house on Friday evening; we'd just left our car there and gone on to the ranch with Olead, because he'd been there before with Jimmy and knew the way. Now, back in Fort Worth, looking at the place by daylight for the first time, I realized again that the definition of the word *mansion*—and Margali Bowman's Ridglea mansion still turned up fairly regularly in magazine and newspaper supplements, described as a major showplace—is a rather elastic one.

Look at it this way: My house has three bedrooms, a living room, a dining ell, a kitchen too small to cuss the cat, much less swing her, two bathrooms, a tiny entry hall, and an enclosed garage. It cost $49,000 when we bought it new, which is too darn much when you consider that it's built of that cheap crumbly Mexican brick they're always warning you about on TV, and the concrete-slab foundation (as we found out only considerably after we moved in) was so badly poured that we have a crack under the dining room carpet that has not only given us a constant problem with ants, but has become so wide that every now and then we find runners of grass protruding out of the floor.

We could sell it now for $65,000. But then we'd have to find another place to live, and we'd probably have to pay at least $75,000 for anything better. Obviously we can't afford that. There are times when I think we can't afford the one we're in.

Margali Bowman and Sam Lang's house—if you believe the magazines—cost them two million dollars. It was indisputably built of the best Acme brick, and it doesn't have a slab foundation. Unusually for Fort Worth, it has a real basement.

Its square footage is probably twice that of our house, if not more, and its location is perfect. It has a separate dining room and breakfast room, a formal living room, a big den, a big kitchen, an indoor swimming pool, and five bathrooms.

Oh, yes, and four bedrooms. One more than my house has. One for Margali, one for Sam, one for Jimmy, and an alleged guest room, which at present was occupied by Darlene, whose exact status in the household I still hadn't figured out for sure.

I was so tired I couldn't see straight. My immediate impulse was to go find Harry and ask him to take me home, but in the first place I hadn't the slightest idea where Harry was, and in the second place I still hadn't had that talk with Fara, who was coming out the front door just as we got out of the limousine.

For that matter, I also hadn't had that talk with Susan, but I could catch her anytime.

Margali walked right past Fara, with a brusque, "Fara, take care of Debra." She breezed on in the front door, leaving Fara standing in the driveway, with a little girl on each side of her, and all three of them staring at me.

"Take care of you? What's she talking about?" Fara asked me. "Do you need a place to change into your swimsuit? We'll have lunch after the swim, of course."

"I'm not going swimming."

"It might be good for you," Susan interrupted behind me. "Really, Deb, swimming in a nice heated pool can't hurt you."

"I'm not going swimming," I repeated, feeling tears alarmingly near the surface. Why hadn't Harry come to see whether I was all right? Was he already in the pool?

Oh, I was being silly. He knew I was all right. "Fara, I got carsick. I need a bath—"

"Oh, you poor thing! Come on, who's got your suitcase? Esther, Dorcas, do you know Olead? He's that nice tall man with brown hair and blue eyes. Go find Olead and ask for Auntie Deb's suitcase."

The little girls, delighted as children always are to help, scampered off, and Fara said, "One thing this house has *plenty* of is bathrooms. But if you need a place to lie down—"

"I do," I interposed.

"I'll find you something."

I was surprised by the determination in her voice, by the sudden take-charge attitude. But on the other hand, this was the first time this weekend I'd seen her away from Edward. Maybe she was less passive without his forbidding presence.

"Deb, you're not feeling sick again?" Susan's voice, behind me, was sharp. "Maybe I should—"

"I'm not sick. I'm just *tired*."

Fara located an unoccupied bathroom and installed me in it. She told me to leave the outer door unlocked and Dolores would come get my clothes and wash them. I did have something clean to put on, didn't I?

I did, Lupe or someone like her having removed Friday-night's clothing while I was watching videotapes, and returned them clean and folded to Saturday-morning's luggage.

Soaking in the bathtub, I was perfectly aware Susan was right. I would feel better after a swim. I probably wouldn't even feel as tired. The reason I wasn't swimming was quite simple.

I didn't—yet—have a maternity swimsuit.

Yes, I've seen photographs, gleefully reproduced in newspapers and magazines, of assorted princesses swimming in bikinis, the ripeness of advanced pregnancy openly displayed.

But I'm not a princess, neither English nor Monacan—Monegasque, somebody told me that was, but I'd certainly never have guessed. I'm a middle-class American, forty-two years old, and those pictures look completely indecent to me.

I wasn't quite into maternity clothes.

All right, I should have been. I'd stretched all my polyester slacks so far that I'd certainly not be able to use them after the baby. But I couldn't show up in maternity clothes until I'd told the captain I was pregnant, and I wasn't ready to do that yet.

But one thing I definitely could not do any longer was get into a size-ten swimsuit.

Somebody knocked on the door. "Deb, are you all right?"

"I'm fine, Fara," I called. "I'll be out in a minute."

"Okay, well, your husband wanted to know."

"Tell him I'm fine." I felt a little better, now that Harry was checking on me.

"And Mother says you can use her room to lie down; she'll be out of it in a minute."

Reluctantly—I could happily have soaked for an hour, and my obstetrician, for reasons best known only to him, has forbidden me the use of a hot tub or sauna for the duration—I climbed out of the bathtub, dried off, and dressed.

Fara, in a swimsuit of startling modesty—the legs came almost to her knees, and formfitting sleeves covered her arms; I couldn't imagine where she had gotten it—was waiting in the hall. "This way," she said.

The door in front of us swung open suddenly, and Margali in a bikini—a sight better imagined than described or seen—strolled out. "Have a nice rest, Debra, dear," she said breezily, as her door closed behind her.

As she went past, not even bothering to speak to her daughter, I noticed she was carrying a glass. It was, of course, filled with an amber fluid and a couple of ice cubes. The smell was not that of iced tea.

"Debra, this is what I wanted you to see," Fara said, and reopened the door.

The master bedroom was approximately the size of the living room *and* the dining ell *and* the kitchen of my house. That was only the bedroom; it didn't include the attached bathroom with step-down tub and a whole wall of linen closets, or the walk-in closet that was somewhat larger than my bedroom.

A pretty white fireplace took up one wall. It hadn't yet been readied for winter, and an arrangement of peacock tails in an Oriental vase sat between two ornate fire dogs.

A California king-size bed, with no headboard or footboard, sat neatly in the center of the room, made up with a gorgeous white fur bedspread.

Other than that, I couldn't decide what the room most resembled—the aftermath of a burglary or the aftermath of an explosion.

□ 4 □

"WHAT IN THE WORLD happened?" I asked.

Every drawer in the large ornate chest of drawers, the long matching dresser, and the matching dressing table with its huge beveled triple mirror was open, contents spilling out onto the floor. Clothes, cosmetics, jewelry, and shoes, along with some assorted magazines, novels, and record jackets, covered almost every square inch of carpet. Except for the cost of the strewn-about items, I'd have thought I was looking at the territory of an unusually untidy teenager.

"Have a look at *this* now," Fara invited, and led me into that vast walk-in closet.

Clothing, from negligees to mink coats, lay strewn on that floor, just as in the bedroom. And shoes—she wasn't much compared to Imelda Marcos, but she certainly could wear a different pair every day for at least a year. About a third of them were either piled in untidy heaps on the floor or thrust higgledy-piggledy back on their shelves so that mates were not together. Fara picked up a white satin evening gown and under it, in the middle of the debris, a floor safe sat open. Setting the gown aside, Fara closed the safe as far as she could without moving the blue cloth that seemed to be caught in the lid, so that I could see a key, attached to a jail-size key ring, protruding from the lock. She reopened it, so that the huge bundle of keys hanging from the same ring jangled discordantly.

"It's always like this," she told me.

"With a house full of servants? Are you serious?"

Fara nodded. "She lets them in here to change the bed and the towels every day. She watches them while they do it. Once a week she lets Dolores get the dirty clothes out of the bedroom and bathroom. Other than that, they're not allowed in here."

"But she used to be—" I stopped, feeling stupid. Of course the contrast between then and now was exactly what had Fara worried. Or at least, part of what had Fara worried.

"I know." Fara nodded. "She used to clean up before the maids arrived so they wouldn't think she was messy. She used to throw a screaming fit if Jimmy or I came down to breakfast without making our beds. She just—she doesn't *care* anymore, Deb."

"That's odd—" I began.

Fara was leaning over, picking up a stole of some long-haired gray fur off the floor. "I'm not sure that's right," she interrupted. "Maybe that's not what I should have said, that she doesn't care. It's—it's as if she can't even *see* this."

"If it's always like this, she probably doesn't see it anymore," I said.

"But how did it *get* to be like this without her seeing it?" Fara shook her head, absently stroking the stole with work-worn hands before wrapping it around a fat blue plastic hanger. "Never mind, you can't answer that any more than I can."

Abruptly she leaned over the safe to pick up the protruding blue cloth. "This isn't supposed to be in here." She held up a small blue velveteen bag, weighed it for a moment in her hand, and then tossed it to me. "Have a look."

I poured the contents out into my hand. Cut but unset gems, scintillating red, green, blue, clear, rainbow. "Good heavens," I said inadequately. I couldn't begin to imagine what they might be worth. Last time I had my engagement ring cleaned, the jeweler told me the stone was now worth about $300; it wasn't a tenth the size of the least one of these diamonds, rubies, emeralds, or sapphires.

"Real?" I asked Fara.

She nodded.

"Margali's?"

"Sam's. He calls them—let's see—a hedge against inflation, or something like that. He says—they're portable. If there was an atomic attack, or a revolution, or something like that, we could walk away with a fortune in our pockets."

With several defense industries located in Fort Worth, if there was an atomic attack, nobody would be walking away. This would be a primary target. But I just nodded. "People have done it before." Pouring the stones back into the bag, I returned it to her.

She accepted it almost reluctantly. "I don't see what good they'd do, in that sort of situation. You can't eat them. In that shape, you can't even wear them. And if you could, they wouldn't keep you warm. But that's Sam. I don't know what they're doing in here. They're supposed to be in Sam's safe. But Mother's a magpie."

Putting the bag back into the safe, she came up with a bundle of papers bound in a torn and faded blue wrapper. Curiously, she opened it. "I thought so. She's been in Sam's safe."

"Oh?" I asked, thinking of a household in which the husband and wife needed separate safes, feeling glad I didn't have one like that.

"This is Mother's will. It's supposed to be in Sam's safe." She was refolding it as she spoke.

"May I see that?" I asked.

Fara handed it to me, a puzzled expression on her face. I didn't open it; she'd already done that, and I'd take her word for it that this was Margali's will. Or, at least, her official will, the one her family knew about.

But it wasn't the one she'd shown me. I didn't have to look at it to know that. It was completely dry, so dry it was almost brittle. And one thing I could be completely sure of was that the will Margali had shown me, wherever it might be right now, was still wet. Not just damp, but out-and-out soaking. And the faded blue of the wrapper on this one, contrasted with the bright blue of the other, told me which was newer.

This wasn't Margali's will. Not anymore.

Fara, sitting on the floor and leaning over, was rummaging down in that metal-cased hole in the floor. "Sam's will is supposed to be—yes—here it is. She's got them both. Or however many there are right now."

I must have looked puzzled, because Fara grimaced. "She's always rewriting her will. She thinks money's what you use to control people, not love, not decency. Just money. Usually the new one sits around the house a day or so and then she throws it in the trash. The one Sam's got—is supposed to have, that is—is supposed to be the official one. She's only supposed to have Sam's and he's supposed to have hers. Oh well, I'll tell him later. He'll come get it back sometime when she's passed out." She sat up, and I handed the other will back to her. Dropping them both into the safe, she closed the lid and removed the key. I followed her back into the bedroom, where she put the immense ring of keys in the top drawer of Margali's dresser. "This is just really secure," she commented, "to keep the key in the room next to the safe."

"Why no combination?" I asked. "Most safes don't have keys at all."

"Can you see Mother getting a combination lock open? It's bad enough when she misplaces the key—this is the only one we've got, because she totally lost the other one. Heaven knows what we'll do if she manages to lose this one. I guess hire a

safecracker. Would you be able to recommend one?" She tried
to laugh.

"The manufacturers would be able to get it open."

Slamming the drawer shut and crossing both arms over it,
Fara turned to me. "But you see what I mean, Deb? She just
doesn't have any idea of security, and—"

"But surely the house has a burglar alarm?" Was that what
Fara was worried about, burglary? Somehow I didn't think so.

"Oh, yes, it has a burglar alarm, wired in with some security
firm," Fara said. She sat down, abruptly, on a corner of the fur-
covered bed. "It has a super-duper good burglar alarm. It also
has an indefinite number of servants who come and go all the
time. She hires them off the street—mostly undocumented al-
iens, I expect—and pays them slave wages." She smiled sadly.
"That's why Jimmy calls all the women Maria and all the men
José. Most of them don't stay long enough for us to get to know
their names. I mean, Mother doesn't even seem to know they're
real. She treats them as if they were robots, with no feelings or
needs whatever. And Sam leaves the running of the household
completely to Mother. And Sanchita, of course."

"Sanchita?"

"The housekeeper. She's been here forever. She's got a little
apartment over the garage. Dolores is her daughter; that's why
even Jimmy doesn't call Dolores Maria."

I sat down beside her. "Then does Sanchita do the actual
hiring of the other servants?"

"Sometimes. But other times Mother does it herself. Right off
the street."

"*Literally* right off—"

Fara grimaced. "Deb, I have been in the car with her and
seen her drive up to a group of men standing on the street corner and tell them to get in the car, that she had work for them.
Honestly, Deb, I have been so embarrassed I could have just
died—I mean, she's tried to hire people off the street and

they've turned out to be business people, or teachers, and one time she was trying to hire a man to come do yard work, and he kept trying to tell her he owned a radio station, and she wasn't even *hearing* him. And of course the ones she gets don't stay; she treats them like dirt and thinks they ought to be grateful for having the chance to work for her."

She paused.

I didn't answer. There didn't seem to be anything to say. We'd gotten rather far afield anyway; this line of thought would be useful if we were investigating a burglary, but we weren't. We were, as best as I could determine, investigating exactly nothing at all.

Then, belatedly, part of what Fara had said registered. "I thought Margali didn't drive herself anymore."

"She's not allowed to. Sam and Mike are supposed to have all the car keys, except for Jimmy's cars, and he's supposed to be very careful to keep his keys away from her. But every now and then she manages to find a set of keys, and every time she does, she's gone."

Silently, I digested that information. Margali had indicated to me that using the chauffeur was her choice, that she was "too nervous" now to drive. But Fara was telling me Margali wasn't allowed to drive, and did so anyway every chance she got.

That was interesting.

Fara shrugged awkwardly. "Deb, I know it was mean of me to ask you here this weekend, knowing what things would be like. But I was afraid you wouldn't believe me if I just told you. And I don't know who to talk to. I just don't know what to do. I think she's crazy. I think my mother's crazy and nobody but me even seems to care!"

"Fara," I asked, "are you asking my advice, or what?"

"I don't know who else to talk to, Deb! I'm sorry, I know you're busy but—"

"It's not that I'm so busy," I told her. "It's just that I can't figure out for sure what it is you want my advice about. If it's burglary prevention—"

Fara sat back slightly and stared at me. "Burglary prevention? Deb, what in the world would I—"

"Fara, what are you asking me about?" I could hear extreme tension in my voice; if it weren't for the fear of being overheard, I might by now have been practically shouting.

"*Mother!*" she replied, and wiped her eyes with the back of her hand. "Deb, what am I going to do about her? I told you, I'm the only one who even cares!"

"You think Sam doesn't?"

She shook her head. "Sam doesn't want to be bothered."

"Fara, he went to the trouble of getting her a very good psychiatrist."

"But he can't go to the trouble of getting the booze away from her."

"That might not be as easy as you think."

"It wouldn't be, of course, but—Oh, Deb!" She ran her fingers through the front of her hair, pulling a little of it loose from its bun. "A psychiatrist, yes, he got her a psychiatrist, but if you'd seen her the day he did that, you'd know why. He was hoping he could manage to get her committed. In a way, so did I; at least she'd be safer there. But—" She shook her head again.

It wasn't necessary to spell that out. In Texas, as in most other places, it has become difficult if not impossible to get a person committed involuntarily, unless it can be conclusively proven that the person's continued freedom constitutes a clear and present danger either to himself or to somebody else.

Courts interpret "clear and present danger" very rigidly. A man who sleeps all night on the street corner in a snowstorm is not, according to that interpretation, a clear and present danger to himself. What it boils down to is that most of the time somebody's dead before you can prove a clear and present danger.

Margali—as long as car keys could be kept away from her—wasn't a danger to anybody but herself. There was no likelihood at all of her becoming violent. And the law as it is presently written grants every adult citizen the legal right to drink himself to death, as long as he can pay for the booze and doesn't get drunk in public.

Ergo, Margali could not be confined to a mental hospital without her own consent, which she certainly was not going to grant.

Nobody wants to go back to the bad old days when just about any minor or female could be committed indefinitely on the word of just about any adult male, but there ought to be some kind of middle ground.

Which brought me to another question—"There isn't a TV show, is there, Fara?" I asked.

Wretchedly, Fara shook her head. "She hasn't even got an agent anymore. When the one she had died, the agency dropped her and she couldn't find a new one to take her on."

"But she honestly believes—"

"I don't know what she believes! I don't know whether she's made it all up herself, or if somebody's feeding her something."

"Feeding her what?" I asked. "PCP? Angel dust?"

Fara stared at me. "What are you talking about?"

"Well, you said—oh!" Now it was my turn to shake my head. "You mean somebody's feeding her something figuratively, not literally. Telling her—"

"What did you *think* I meant? Oh, that story about somebody poisoning her?" Fara wasn't facing me; she was looking down at her hands, which were tracing aimless little patterns on the thick white fur—mink? ermine?—that covered the bed. "That was the day Sam got the psychiatrist. He was really trying to get her locked up. And she kept screaming and acting—"

"You think she made it up?" I interrupted.

Fara shook her head. "I don't know what I think. About that,

I just don't know what to think. I mean, there was no doubt she was really sick, but—" She stopped, continuing to shake her head. Was it some kind of nervous habit? Did she even know she was doing it?

"But what?" I finally prompted.

"Who *would*? And why?"

"She told me it was because of her will. She kept saying 'they.' And then she said 'they' were Sam and Jimmy and you. But then when I asked her whether she thought you and Sam and Jimmy were trying to kill her, she said no. And then she said, not Fara." But her reason for removing Fara from the list, I remembered suddenly, was rather ephemeral. Technically I was betraying a confidence. But—

All right. Whether I was right or wrong, I thought Fara had the right to know what was going on. Fara. Not Jimmy, whom I totally distrusted and even, in some vague and undefinable way, feared, or Sam, whom I didn't know, but Fara. Especially since she was asking my advice. I didn't have any advice to give her. But at least I could tell her what little I knew.

"She said Sam and Jimmy and I were trying to kill her because of her will? Oh, Deb, that's absurd! She hasn't got anything to leave. Anyway, I told you, she's always changing her will."

"She what?" Involuntarily I looked around the room, stuck on the next-to-the-last statement. "What do you mean, nothing to leave?"

"Everything she's got is Sam's. She made a lot of money, sure, in her day and for her day, but she spent it as fast as it came in and then some. My father's money is in a trust fund; proceeds of it went to her till I was out of high school, and then it came to me. The whole thing was set up as soon as he and Mother were married."

That was a little surprise—dowdy, subservient Fara, the sole heiress to an Arab oil fortune? But she was still talking.

"Jimmy's father was like Margali; he spent everything as fast as it came in—"

"Who was Jimmy's father?" I vaguely remembered Jimmy's birth, but I was only fifteen. That was a lot of years ago. I hadn't the slightest idea who Margali had been married to that particular year. Somebody named Messick, I surmised, but that was all I could guess.

Fara grimaced again. "Oh, I hated him. Sunny Messick. He drove a race car. Mother married him when I was thirteen and he used to feel me up all the time whenever he got me alone. I didn't know what to do about it."

She wouldn't, of course. If Margali was a natural-born victim, Fara was even more so.

"She broke up with him after a year or so. Then they had this grand reunion just before some big race and they were out there hanging all over each other at the racetrack and then he went and got in his car and gave her that thumbs-up signal, you know, and took off, and he was staying in the lead and it looked like he was going to win, and then on the next to the last lap he spun out real bad and his car rolled over about forty-nine times and caught on fire." She shuddered. "I was there. I remember. I hated him, but not that much. They had this grand funeral for him up at Forest Lawn. You remember, Deb, you went with me."

And suddenly I did remember—sloping hills covered with incredibly green grass, grave markers set flush in the grass, no tombstones anywhere, but an occasional statue standing around here and there, and Margali swathed in black, weeping, leaning on—"Leaning on Sam!" I said aloud. "Sam was at the funeral? Or do I remember wrong?"

Fara nodded. "He was there. That's the first time I remember meeting him. And then the next thing I knew Margali was pregnant and everybody was making this great big fuss over the posthumous child of the great Sunny Messick. I don't know what was so great about him. It was the car that did all the work."

Having had to drive a lot faster than I wanted to several times myself, I had to laugh at that. "Well, the driver does do some work too, Fara. But anyhow—"

"Well, I don't know anything about that. Just, Sunny was always trying to feel me up and then Sunny was dead. And that was the only race I ever went to and I'll never go to another."

"Okay." I was trying to get things straight in my mind. Not that there was likely to be a connection, but you never know what buried trauma will trigger odd behavior. Of course all this was Susan's job, not mine, but—

All right, call me nosy. "Was it right after Jimmy was born that Sam and Margali were married?"

"Uh-uh," Fara said. "It wasn't until I got out of high school."

"So there wasn't any possibility, say, that Jimmy could have been Sam's—"

"What a silly question." Fara flopped over backward on the bed, feet still on the floor and hands lying back above her head. "No. I said right after the funeral, but of course she was pregnant before the race. She just wasn't showing. But Jimmy was born, let's see, about five months after the race. And he was a full-term baby. That wasn't why she married Sam. It was because I was out of high school."

~That didn't seem to make sense. I didn't speak, and after a while Fara said, "You don't see the connection, do you?"

"No," I said.

"She was through by then. As an actress, I mean. She wasn't making any more movies, and she didn't have a cent left of that fortune she'd made. She'd spent all of mine the guardians would let her, but she couldn't have that money anymore because I was out of high school and it was mine. Deb, I told her I'd pay for a house and utilities and one car and food and medical expenses, that sort of thing, all the bills reasonable people reasonably have. But I wasn't going to throw my money after hers on fourteen servants and twenty-nine cars and three fur coats every year for her. There wasn't any reason why I should."

"Of course not." And I wondered how that hardheaded Fara had turned into the woman I saw around Edward Johnson.

"I mean, sure, it's a lot of money, but it's not inexhaustible. And the oil prices, you know, you never know what they're going to do. It's *my* money. I don't mind taking care of her within reason, but, well, you know what I mean."

I wondered how much of that money was going now to the Evangelical Church of—whatever.

I didn't ask.

Fara went on talking, almost compulsively. "So she had enough to live on like a normal human being—I made sure of that—but it wasn't enough. Not for her. I mean, she could spend forty thousand dollars a year just on flowers that she'd never even bother to smell or look at. So she married Sam. They split up once more, but she came right back. He still loved her then. He'd been asking her to marry him, and he had plenty of money. And still has. So you see, Deb, she hasn't got anything to leave. Not to anybody. Even the jewels she wears really belong to Sam."

I tried to think of something, anything, that could bring this into any kind of sensible focus. There's been quite a revival of old movies lately. "Residuals, or royalties, or whatever they call it? Anything like that?"

Fara shook her head for about the twentieth time. "Residuals. But she hasn't got any. I kind of think she might have had a lousy agent, but I don't know for sure. Anyway, she hasn't got any. I'm telling you, Deb, she hasn't got anything to leave. So there's sure no reason to poison her over a will, no matter what—delusions she's got. They're *her* delusions. The rest of us know. Even Jimmy—he's freaky, but he knows Margali hasn't got anything to give him. It's Sam and me he mooches from. Except for that one time he decided to be an actor. Now, that was a laugh. Or at least it would have been if I hadn't had to buy the director off."

"What?"

"Oh, I don't want to talk about it." She sat up straight. "I'm sorry, Deb, you wanted to rest and here I've been telling you all my problems. I should have waited until—"

"Oh, that's okay," I said tritely. "After all, what are friends for?"

"Not to keep each other awake when they're feeling bad, that's for sure. I'll see to it somebody calls you for lunch."

After she left, I lay back gingerly on the bedspread. I couldn't manage Fara's casual sprawl. It somehow did not feel proper to be lying on mink. Improper, but exceedingly comfortable, I then decided drowsily.

A moment later I began to remember that when the kids were little they thought if I was taking a nap and they woke me up by whispering instead of screaming "Hey, Mom!", it didn't count as disturbing me.

It wasn't the kids whispering to me now. It was Susan. She was disturbing me all the same. I said "Huh" or something equally intelligent.

"Are you awake?"

"Uh-huh." I did not sit up. I did, however, go to the length of opening both eyes instead of just one, which is what I normally do for the children when they disturb my naps.

"How much of that Coke or whatever it was did you drink?"

"Ah, Susan, not again!" I protested.

"Deb, I've got to know." She sounded somewhat odd, and I did a little more than open my eyes. I actually looked at her.

She did not look like her normal cool, unruffled self.

I sat up. "What'd you do, call the lab and tell them to rush it?"

"Sometimes waiting isn't such a good idea."

"It must not be too bad. You haven't called an ambulance or anything. Have you?"

"Uh-uh. Deb, how much of it did you drink?"

"I don't know. Maybe half, maybe a third, maybe not that much. I told you it didn't taste right. What was in it, Susan?"

One of her braids was on its way down on the right, and distractedly, she started pulling more bobby pins out. "Traces. Just traces."

"Just traces of *what*? What is this, a quiz show?"

"Traces of copper, barium, selenium, lead, thallium, arsenic, and antimony."

"*What*? Susan, what's this going to do to my baby? What—"

"Nothing. Almost certainly nothing. I mean, you didn't shake the can up or anything—"

"What in the world would I be shaking a soda pop up for—Susan, what are you—"

"It's heavy metal. They're all heavy metal. They don't dissolve. And that's what—whoever it was—didn't think about. They were put in there heaven knows when; as you said, the can might have sat out there all summer. And they settled. They settled down to the bottom of the can and you just drank what was on top. And most of them—especially the copper—irritate the digestive tract. Badly. If you still had any of it in you, you'd still be vomiting. So you got rid of all of it. But there's no way at all of knowing how much was in the can, not from what we've got to go on now. I've sent a couple of Parker County deputy sheriffs back up there to try to find the can."

"Without a search warrant."

"Well. They can say please, can't they?"

"Yes, and do you think Lupe or whoever else is up there—"

"The housekeeper. You never did meet her."

"Do you think the housekeeper is going to turn the can over to the deputy sheriff? And it'll be all just dandy if she does?"

"Why wouldn't she? And what would be wrong if—"

"Susan. She doesn't have the authority."

"Oh." Susan was repinning the braid. She fidgets with her braids more than I've ever seen anybody else fidget with anything. "I didn't think of that."

"Of course you didn't. You're not a cop."

"But why wouldn't she have the authority? She's Sam's designated representative up there, isn't she?"

"Yeah. Oh well, maybe, but—"

"Look," Susan interrupted vigorously, "you're right, I'm not a cop. I'm a doctor and—"

"And I'm not your patient."

"No, damn it, but you're my *friend*. And anyway if it was aimed at Margali—Margali *is* my patient."

"Do you suppose that's what she got the first time?"

"I don't know. It could have been."

"What all was it you said again?" I was wide awake now, more awake than I'd been in days, maybe weeks. It was, I knew perfectly well, the rush of adrenaline. When it faded, it was going to leave me even more tired than I had been before.

"Traces of copper, barium, selenium, lead, thallium, arsenic, and antimony."

"Why wouldn't the arsenic show up on the test you did in your lab?"

"It was only a trace. Too little to find with the test I used, and believe me, the test I used could find an *extremely* sublethal dose. The crime lab used neutron-activation analysis. And that'll find *anything*."

"Where in the heck did he—whoever—manage to come up with a concoction like that anyway?" I demanded, with an idiotic sense of outrage.

"The lab man told me that stuff is used as fire salts."

"Fire salts? What in the world are fire salts?"

"Oh, you know," Susan said. "That stuff you sprinkle on a fire to make it burn more brightly, with all kinds of pretty colors in the flame, green for copper, blue for—oh, I don't know. And I guess the next question is, where did they come from?"

"Open your eyes," I said.

The fireplace, there in Margali's room, was as I said not ready yet for winter. Peacock feathers and an Oriental vase took the place of logs. But nobody had ever removed the matches. There they sat on one corner of the hearth, a nice ornamental box filled with nice long ornamental fireplace matches, the kind that don't strike worth a darn, so you have to light them with something else before you can use them to light the wood in the fireplace. Or, actually, the paper you light to light the wood.

Right beside the matches was a pretty blue and green box that looked like the sprinkly kind of talcum powder. A round box, narrower than a salt box and taller. Kind of the shape of those Avon talcum powders they sell to parents for their kids to give to teachers for Christmas.

And on the box it said, "FireBrite Ornamental Fire Salts."

On the back label was a warning: "Not to be taken internally; if accidentally taken internally, induce vomiting and call nearest Poison Control Center."

"And of course it's perfectly simple how to get it in the can," I said.

"It is?" Susan is not constantly around males tinkering with things. "I mean, I can see using a hypodermic or something like that to get the powder into the drink, but then you'd have a leak."

"Not if you patched it with solder," I replied. "It'd take about five minutes to heat the soldering iron and about two seconds to mend the hole."

"Only then the drink would get flat."

"Which it did, Susan," I pointed out. "Which it did."

"Which might have saved your life. Oh, hell," Susan said, "I should have gotten you to the hospital as soon as you started puking."

"If you took every pregnant woman who started puking to the hospital, you sure would need a big hospital."

"Oh, I know it," Susan said, flinging herself distractedly down on the end of the bed, cowboy boots and all. "But—"

"But nothing. Okay. The day Margali got sick, do you know whether she had been up to the ranch? I mean, we need to know whether that's the only place the stuff is, or whether—"

"She'd been to the ranch. She started puking halfway back to Fort Worth."

"What had she been drinking? Or do you know?"

"I know. I asked. Rum and Coke. That good old Cuba Libre. Only for her it was always Diet Coke."

"Was anybody else drinking rum and Coke? Diet or regular? Or did you ask that?"

"I asked. No. She was up there by herself except for the housekeeper."

"The housekeeper lives there. It's not Sanchita; it's somebody else. All right, if she went up there alone, how'd she get there?"

"Alone except for the chauffeur. And you've known her a lot longer than I have—did you ever know her to drink with the hired hands?"

"There's that," I agreed. "But Susan, we've got to do something fast or next time it will work."

"He's so bloody careless," Susan brooded.

"He? Poison is more often a female crime."

"So? If it's a woman, who did it? That wet dishrag Fara Johnson."

"Fara's no wet dishrag."

"Oh, I know she's not, but when I see her waiting hand and foot on that nasty-minded little twit of a husband of hers, I just get so mad."

"She thinks it's her religious duty. I think."

"Anyway, do you think she did it?"

"No, I don't think Fara did anything she shouldn't. But—"

"All right, so who are you going to tell? Fara? Sam? Jimmy, for crying out loud?"

"What's with Jimmy, anyway?" I asked.

Susan shrugged, which is hard to do when you're lying on your stomach on a mink bedspread. "Professional or personally?"

"Huh?"

"If you're asking my professional opinion, severe and unresolved problems of—problems of—Deb, if I tried to tell you, you wouldn't understand one word in ten, and I don't have the legal right to tell you anyway."

"Personally then. In my language."

"In your language—in your very own language—the boy's a bloody fruitcake. And that means exactly nothing and you know it as well as I do."

"I never called anybody a bloody fruitcake in my life. A fruitcake, maybe, but not a bloody one. Anyway, does that make him capable of—"

"How can anybody say what anyone else is capable of? He might be. He probably is. I just don't see any reason why he would, that's all."

"You know the family, don't you?" I asked.

"Oh, yeah. Jimmy's been a patient of the clinic about fourteen years, off and on."

"So you kind of know the situation."

"I kind of know the situation."

"So what is the situation? As you see it, I mean. Nonprofessionally," I added hastily, afraid she'd clam up again.

"The situation as I see it. Nonprofessionally. All right. Sam fell head-over-heels in love with a pretty face. He married it and it unmarried him and first chance he got he married it back, only the face sort of got unpretty. Okay? But Sam's a Catholic and he doesn't believe in divorce and anyway work is his mistress; there's nobody waiting in the wings, if you know what I mean. And Jimmy—in layman's parlance—is three-thirds of a squirrel and to my mind, whether you agree or not, Fara's a wet dishrag. Okay. I sound unsympathetic and unprofessional and I know it and I wouldn't say any of this to anybody but you, and if you ask me to repeat it in court I'll categorically deny every word of it. Damn it, Deb, it would take about nineteen different kinds of medication plus about ten years of family therapy to make this family even begin to function as a family, and obviously there aren't ten years available and each of them thinks the whole problem is somebody else's fault and none of them ever want to take prescriptions. They all take them about three days and then stop. It's enough—almost enough—to drive *me* to drink. But what you were asking—Fara and Sam have all the money, so there's nobody to leave any to Jimmy. And—Deb, there is no earthly reason why anyone would want to murder Margali. At least not that I know of. And whoever did it is damn careless anyway."

"Agreed."

"I mean, just putting the stuff in a soda pop can, anybody could have gotten it, even one of those kids—"

"Fara would realize that," I said. "Fara wouldn't have put the stuff in the can. But—"

"But would Edward realize it? Is that what you were wondering?"

"Yeah, I guess. Partly anyway."

"Maybe not," Susan said, "but why would Edward want to kill Margali?"

"Susan," I said, "why would anybody?" A thought suddenly occurred to me. "Would Margali be capable—in your opinion—of pulling this herself to get attention."

"Absolutely," Susan answered promptly.

At that moment the door opened and Fara came in, halting abruptly when she saw I wasn't alone. "Oh, hello, Susan," she said. "Deb, I came to tell you lunch is ready."

I didn't exactly think I wanted to eat. From the expression on Susan's face, I suspected she agreed.

But it ought to be all right. He wouldn't want to poison us all. Would he? Or she—whoever he or she was?

And why didn't I, right then, make an official report?

Because right then, at that point, until the can turned up, we still didn't have any evidence that a crime had been committed. Sure, I could call my office and tell my captain, and he'd say, "Where's your evidence?" and I'd say "Oh, er, ah . . ."

I'd wait, I'd decided, until the can was found and examined, so that we'd have the puncture mark and the solder we had to have, and whatever had settled in the bottom of the can.

And then I'd get Margali out of that house. Some way or another, even if I had to invite her to come spend a week with me (oh joy, oh bliss!), I'd get her out of that house until I found out who was trying to kill her.

In the meantime, Susan agreed, she'd have Darlene—a very competent psychiatric nurse, on leave from Braun Clinic to look after Margali—examine everything that Margali alone was eating or drinking. It might drive Margali crazy, but if the nurse assured her it was to protect her from poison, she might feel flattered instead of annoyed.

That's what we decided.

It wasn't very smart.

·5·

WHY HADN'T I noticed when I was a child, a teenager, how bad Margali's taste was? But I knew the answer to that. I hadn't because she was rich and we were poor; she was a movie star and my dad was a milkman and my mom was a housewife, and so whatever Margali did, whatever Margali bought, must be the right thing to do or buy, because Margali must know.

I looked, now, at the furniture Margali considered appropriate for the dining room of a Fort Worth town house, and wondered how Sam could stand it. Did he just not notice, or was it worth the eyestrain to him to avoid quarreling with her?

None of it was cheap. All of it was of the very best possible quality. But not a single piece matched, or in any way coordinated with, anything else, and absolutely nothing was in any way appropriate to the Southwestern image the outside of the house projected.

Showplace, I thought. No wonder the magazines show only the outside of this house.

The table was mahogany. I don't know what you call that design; it looked very fancy and ornate and European, with feet like eagles' claws festooned with grapes and pineapples. Margali had partially covered the glossy surface with Irish-linen place mats.

The sideboard also was mahogany, but it was from a completely different period. It had an almost Shaker-like simplicity that showed off the beautiful grain of the red wood far better than the ornate carving of the table did.

Over the sideboard was an English-style oil painting—very dark—of some kind of whitish retriever with brownish spots carrying a dead pheasant proudly in its mouth. The dog had huge brown soulful eyes, the kind my half pit bull, half Doberman Pat gets when he's contemplating eating the mail carrier. The pheasant was bleeding. Badly. There was blood dripping from the dog's mouth and puddling onto the ground.

Gross, I thought. As my sixteen-year-old would put it, grossamundo. I averted my eyes, far later than I should have done, to the assorted serving pieces of silver and gold that littered the sideboard. They were all very carefully polished, without a trace of tarnish anywhere on them. They were strewn in no apparent order across the polished wood, and one of them—some kind of large serving dish—contained a huge pile of what looked at first glance like plastic fruit but probably was actually some horribly expensive French or Italian glass import I wasn't rich enough to know about.

Margali—or Sam—or whoever had the money—probably wasn't any better off than my son-in-law Olead Baker, who had somehow in the seven years since he turned twenty-one parlayed the two million dollars he'd inherited from his father into quite a lot more. I didn't know how much more; I didn't ask, because it wasn't any of my business. But I was quite sure he could buy everything Margali and Sam had in this house and never notice a gap in his checkbook.

But Olead didn't live like this. His and Becky's house was sane, coordinated, pleasant.

Even Olead's mother and her second husband, who didn't have anywhere near Olead's sense, hadn't lived like this. Some of their belongings were inappropriately elaborate, but they all fit together into a reasonably pleasant if overformal whole.

And why was I concentrating so hard on the furniture, the pictures on the wall, the array of metal on the sideboard? Because if I concentrated on that, I might not have to hear what was going on in the way of conversation. Sam was sniping at Margali; Margali was sniping at Jimmy; everybody was sniping at everybody, except Bob Campbell and Carl Hendricks, who seemed to be ignoring the entire commotion, and Darlene Cooney and Susan Braun, who were carrying on some sort of private conversation at their own corner of the table.

Oh, I suppose that summary isn't quite accurate. Becky and Olead were carrying on a quiet conversation of *their* own; Harry was staring at the table; and the two little girls, mercifully, had been removed by a maid and presumably were having a quietly pleasant luncheon in another room, away from their grandmother as well as their father.

Not that our lunch wasn't delicious. It was far more sensibly planned and presented than breakfast; probably that was because the housekeeper—what was her name, Sanchita?—was more capable of sensible planning than Margali, or whomever she'd delegated to think up that idiotic country breakfast. There was some sort of flame-roasted chicken, boneless, that tasted as if it had been marinated in pineapple juice; a light salad of avocado and tomatoes; an Oriental-tasting rice salad that was a happy choice with the chicken; and a relish plate. For the first time that day, my stomach wasn't complaining.

My stomach—and the rice salad—were the only things that were happy.

Certainly nobody at the table was.

"Why aren't you eating your lunch, Marjorie?" Sam inquired. "Or do you want to tell us *this* is poisoned? The rest of us seem to be doing just fine."

"Having *some* people around would poison *any* meal," Margali returned, in her most dulcet tones. "Jimmy, dear, don't you think a fork would work better on the rice?"

"My third birthday wasn't last week. I'll eat however I please."

I didn't say anything. This time, however, I sided with Margali. Jimmy was holding the spoon like a shovel, and the sight was not pretty.

I looked at Harry. Harry did not look at me.

That was probably just as well. After all, these were supposed to be *my* friends.

Edward Johnson said something to Fara about a revival meeting they would be missing that night if they went to the Blue Owl.

Fara said something about her mother's birthday coming only once a year, and pointed out that they went to revival meetings almost every night.

Well, well, Fara, I thought, is the worm turning? Hurrah, hurrah!

Edward muttered, "Leave the dead to bury their dead," and Susan glanced around at him quickly.

"What did you say?" she asked.

"It's a quotation from the Holy Scriptures. I certainly wouldn't expect you to recognize it."

"Actually I do. But I'm not sure you've applied it accurately."

"My dear woman, I have several degrees in theology. I'm quite sure I know what—"

"But do you read Greek?"

"Do I what?"

"Do you read Greek?"

"Well, I—"

"Susan, what *is* it in Greek?" I had to ask.

Susan smiled sweetly. "Oh, it's exactly the same thing. But I don't think it has anything whatever to do with whether or not Fara should keep her promise to attend all of her mother's birthday party."

"The Lord didn't—"

"He ate with sinners and publicans. He blessed the wedding at Cana. Edward Johnson, I don't think I like your church." Susan rose and swept away from the table.

Margali stared after her, and then turned to me. "Debra, dear, what was it Edward said? I didn't quite catch—"

"Why don't you ask Edward?" Jimmy interrupted, wiping several grains of rice from his mouth with the back of his hand.

"Edward, dear, what was it you said?"

"Never mind," Edward said, and stood abruptly. "All right, Fara, we'll stay tonight, but that's it; we have to be in Tyler by—"

"We'll be there," Fara said, once more the meek servant of the servant.

Margali stood now too, confounding a small slim dark woman—Oriental, this time, instead of Mexican—who was entering with a tray of bowls filled with what looked like lime sherbet. "And now I have a special, special treat for you," Margali cooed. "It's in the den—dear, would you serve the dessert in the den instead of in here?"

The servant looked puzzled. "Ma'am?"

"In the den," Margali said, somewhat more loudly.

"Marjorie, nobody understands English any better shouted than spoken," Sam said impatiently. He motioned to the servant to return to the kitchen. "Sanchita will explain." The servant continued to look puzzled. "Sanchita," Sam repeated.

The servant nodded vigorously. "Sanchita," she agreed, and at last turned to carry the sherbet back to the kitchen.

"What's the treat, Mother?" Fara asked. I noted a tone of resignation in her voice; she must have suspected what was coming.

"My Academy Award-winning film—"

"Ah, shit, Mother!" Jimmy said loudly, drowning out the rest of her sentence. "The only thing that dog won an award for was best titles!"

"Jimmy, they don't give awards for—"

"Jimmy, you don't have to be so—"

Margali and Fara were drowning each other out, and Sam shouted, "All right, Marjorie, but give people a choice, can't you? I mean, some people don't want to spend their lives watching old movies!"

"I could look at that sweet little lady all day," Carl Hendricks said, "but happens I got me a business meeting at the Petroleum Club and I'm way past due." He looked pointedly—and belatedly—at his watch, and added, "So I'll have to be excused."

Bob Campbell sat resignedly. Carl was Sam's business partner, but Bob was Margali's attorney—whatever it was she needed an attorney for—and probably it wasn't as easy for him to bow out as it was for Carl.

Apparently the meal was considered finished. I looked sadly at my departing chicken; I could have eaten a lot more of it. But I'm an obedient guest. I followed Margali as she strode out of the room.

And following her, I got the full impact of her after-swimming costume for the first time. She was now wearing a red miniskirt, a white middy blouse with red polka dots and puffed sleeves, and red ballet slippers laced with ribbons that crisscrossed up to her knees.

Her husband and children didn't seem to notice anything unusual in her attire, which I guess said something about her. Or them. Or both.

The den, at least, was sensibly furnished, with comfortable rather than elegant chairs. Instead of the television and VCR we'd used last night on the ranch, we had a real movie screen and projector, in a little projection room at the back of the den. I couldn't see who was running the projector—another José or Maria, most likely.

The lime sherbet, which arrived in the den about the same time we did, was frosty, but it left me thirsty. There was a little bar-style refrigerator in a corner of the room, and Margali, now sprawled elegantly on a silk-covered chaise lounge, gestured lazily toward it. "Something to drink?" she asked the room at large.

"Yes, thanks," I said, and bent over the refrigerator. Bending, I noticed, wasn't as easy as it used to be.

The refrigerator contained a lot of mixers, quinine water (my doctor has absolutely forbidden me quinine water for the duration), a lot of beer and *cerveza*, which of course is Mexican beer, and at the back, a few Diet Cokes and Diet Sprites. I took a Diet Coke. It was good and cold; apparently it had been chilling quite a while.

I was glad it was cold. I was feeling drowsy again.

"Deb, let me see that," Susan said, behind me.

I handed it to her, suddenly a little less drowsy.

Casually, she turned it around in her hand.

Casually, she moved out of the dimly lit den, where the projectionist was focusing the numbers on the screen, into the brightly lighted hall behind it.

Casually, I followed her.

She turned the can so that I could see what she had found.

There it was, at the seam, toward the bottom—a spot of solder. Not a large spot. Just large enough. Just large enough to cover the mark that might be made by a hypodermic needle going through the seam.

"That's it, Deb," Susan said quietly to me. "Do you take charge, or do I?"

"We haven't tested it yet. And if we create a panic—"

"We don't need to create a panic. We just need to make sure nobody drinks—"

"I can handle that," I said. I went back into the den and leaned over Fara. "Fara," I said, "I need your help."

"What?"

"Will you come out to the hall?"

She followed me. Nobody else paid any attention; the movie was starting, and what it lacked in quality, it made up for in loudness. It had begun in the middle of a battle between the French Foreign Legion and some kind of attacking Arab contingent mounted on screaming horses that for some reason kept falling down. Loudly.

"Fara," I said, "somebody might really be trying to poison your mother."

"What?"

"Look." Susan pointed to the dot of solder on the can.

Fara followed her finger. "So? What has that got to do with—"

"Never mind now. Just say it doesn't belong there. We've got to get every can of soft drink out of that refrigerator and out of every other place your mother uses to stash drinks, and examine every one of them."

Fara was subservient, but she wasn't stupid, no matter what Susan thought. "Deb," she said, "when you got sick today—"

"When I got sick, I'd been drinking one of Margali's Diet Cokes. And Susan had some tests run."

"But Deb, shouldn't you be in the hospital then?"

"Susan says it wasn't enough to hurt me. But I didn't drink as much of it as your mother would, because I—when I drink soda pop, I just drink soda pop. I don't mask the taste. It didn't taste right to me. I didn't finish it. But—"

"But if you had poured in a triple jigger of whiskey you wouldn't notice the taste. But—good heavens—" She revolved, slowly, staring at the den, her sallow face paling. "Right there in the den—the girls could—"

Then it hit me. They don't drink coffee. They don't drink tea. "Would the girls have had any kind of Cokes? Diet or regular?"

"Oh, no," she answered mechanically, "I don't let them have anything with caffeine in it, but—"

"You and Edward don't use caffeine either?"

"No, but the Sprites—"

"Does Jimmy drink Diet Cokes? Or Sam?"

"Jimmy hates them. He says they don't taste right without sugar. And Sam just drinks Scotch and water."

"So no resident or usual guest in this household except Margali would ever drink Diet Cokes."

Fara stared at me. "No, I used to drink a lot of Cokes, but then I quit using caffeine and I got where I couldn't handle a lot of sugar, and by the time they came out with the sugar-free, caffeine-free Cokes, I was out of the habit and I just never did get back into it. But I let the girls have Sprite and 7-Up and Slice—"

"But I don't think the Sprite and 7-Up and Slice are going to have anything in them," Susan said slowly. "No. I see what you're getting at, Deb. It's brilliant—whoever thought it up— it's brilliant, because she drinks all the time, we would check the booze, but she uses a lot of different mixers, and would we think to check them? Any of them? The cans, or anything left in the cans?"

"We wouldn't get the chance," I answered. "We'd never get the chance, because by the time anybody got here to check it, that can wouldn't be here. All that'd be here would be a nice innocent can that never had anything in it—a nice innocent can that would have Margali's fingerprints on it. Real easy to get."

"But what can we *do*?" Fara asked. "How can we protect her?"

"Right now, think of some excuse. Tell her we've found out there's a batch of bad drinks or something, and get all the Diet Cokes out of the refrigerator in there—that'll be a start. She'll wonder what's going on if Susan or I do it, but you can."

"Yes. That'll be okay for now. For this moment. But what if you're wrong? What if it's in the other cans too?"

Susan showed her what to look for.

"But even so—what good'll it do? I mean, whoever did it is probably right there in that room, he'll know—"

"We'll have to find out, of course," I said. "But for now Darlene'll be careful, and it shouldn't take us long. There'll be fingerprints."

There would be. Mine. And Susan's. And Fara's. And probably nobody else's. And I hadn't the faintest idea what I was going to do to find out who it was who had doctored the cans. But I was going to have to find out, and soon, before he—or she—decided to doctor something else.

Yes, we were warning the would-be killer, probably, because Fara was almost certainly right that whoever did it was in the den watching Margali's movies. But whether we warned him or not, we had to get the doctored cans out of the den before somebody—anybody—drank one of them.

Fara bypassed Margali completely. She just made a quick, shrewd check of the room to make sure nobody had taken a Diet Coke—nobody had—and then she knelt composedly in front of the little refrigerator, ignoring the shrieks from the screen as the beautiful redhead—Margali of forty years ago—was borne away on the beautiful white stallion of a brown-faced, hawk-nosed, burnoosed chieftain with strikingly beautiful bright blue eyes.

A moment later Margali, unmoved by the hysteria of her screen image, said crossly, "Fara, can't you close that thing? It's letting too much light into the room."

"In a minute, Mother," Fara said. "I'm looking for something."

"Then look faster."

"I'll be through in just a minute."

She went on sorting through cans.

"Do you trust her?" Susan asked me, very quietly. "Fara, I mean?"

I nodded. "I've known her thirty-five years. You get to know someone pretty well in that long a time."

"What about that husband of hers?"

I grimaced and shrugged. "But if he was doing it, he wouldn't tell her," I added. "Fara loves her mother. Heaven knows why—Margali is nicer to the dogs than she is to Fara—but she does. And he's smart enough to know it. And he knows who's got the money."

Fara shut the door of the little refrigerator and rose to her feet, with five cans of Diet Coke in her hands.

Margali's eyes followed her, and there was a look in them any experienced cop learns to know—the look of somebody who's getting away with something. The con man who's pulled it off this time.

Susan, beside me, was as still as I was. She wouldn't miss that expression.

"What are you doing with those?" Edward asked irritably, noticing the cans Fara was holding.

"Taking them to Deb."

"Why?" His angry gaze shifted to me.

"Because she asked me to."

"Maybe?" Susan asked me, glancing quickly at Edward.

"Maybe," I agreed. "But I don't think so."

"I don't either."

"I think he's just afraid she'll feed caffeine to the children."

"I wouldn't feed caffeine to my children if I had any," Susan answered. "And I wish to goodness you'd quit feeding caffeine to that little one."

"What little one? My daughters are married and Hal is six feet tall." Presumably his Korean forebears had been short, as Koreans usually are, but somewhere in his genes there must be a giant. His pediatrician was gloomily predicting he'd top out somewhere around six feet nine.

I was not looking forward to buying him shoes when he got to be six feet nine. They were costing quite enough already.

"*That* little one." Susan indicated my midsection.

Fara heard her. "Debra, are you pregnant?"

"Yeah, I'm pregnant," I muttered.

"Why, that's wonderful! Congratulations!" Fara, as an old friend, had suffered with me through a lot of times when I wasn't pregnant. "Oh, it's all right, isn't it? I mean, your age and everything?"

"It's all right. And Fara, please don't talk about it; it's still a secret, okay? And right now we need to think about—"

"Oh. Yeah." Fara looked back down at the cans she was balancing.

I took one out of her hands and turned it around. There it was, on the seam toward the bottom of the can, the single dot of solder.

"Just the Diet Coke cans?" Susan asked.

Fara nodded. "You were right. All the others were all right, at least so far as I could tell."

Sam was suddenly standing in the doorway, looming over us. "What are you saying? Who was all right?"

We all jumped; we must have looked as guilty as Macbeth's three witches. Susan found her voice first. "Deb. She's still not feeling all right. You know she got sick."

Sure, throw me to the wolves, I thought crossly. But I tried to look wan, which wasn't easy when I was as wound up as I was right then, and said, "I'm really okay, but—" I made my voice sound weak, so that I didn't sound okay.

Sometimes I think I'm a pretty good actress.

Sam looked very sympathetic. "Well, ladies, do you really think five Diet Cokes will help any? Or six?" He'd just spotted the one that Susan was holding.

Susan shrugged. "Who knows?"

"Don't you think it might be a good idea for her to go and lie down?"

"A very good idea," Susan said. "If she gets sick much more, we might need to think about just running a few tests."

Was that some kind of warning to Sam, that if he was the one who had doctored the cans, he'd better see to it I didn't drink one? I didn't think so. If it was, it didn't work. He just offered me some ice, which I refused, and then said he'd find me a place to lie down.

Leaving Susan and Fara to stare at each other and try to think up a topic of conversation that might explain what they were doing standing in the hall juggling six cans of pop, I meekly followed Sam down the hall. I turned once to look questioningly at Susan; she gave me a thumbs-up signal. She had the situation under control, I guess.

Sam didn't take me back to Margali's bedroom; instead he took me to his own. It was far and away the most sensible room I'd seen in the house thus far. It had, like Margali's room, a California king-size bed, but it was covered with a plaid bedspread, and instead of ornate draperies, his windows were covered only with miniblinds. His walk-in closet was smaller and far neater than Margali's, his bathroom had a tub and shower instead of a wading pool, and his dresser and chest of drawers coordinated with his bed.

A wall safe was standing open above the dresser. Sam followed my gaze, chuckled, and closed it, so that the mirror that made up its outer cover was again visible. "I just can't get used to a little thing like you being a police officer," he said. "Sure, I guess the first thing you think when you see something standing open like that is how easy it would be to get in it."

"I'm afraid I do," I agreed. "I mean, I've worked so many burglaries, and—"

"We never bother to lock it," Sam said flatly. "The man I bought it from, he told me it wasn't no good as a safe. He told me a good safe man'd get it open quicker'n I can open it with a key."

"That's perfectly true, I'm sorry to say. So in that case why bother with it at all?" I didn't tell him that a good safe man can get just about *any* safe open faster than the owner could open it with a key. I've seen a top-grade Mossler gaping open, spilling fireclay and looking like a sardine can somebody had ripped open with an old-fashioned blade can opener, when the burglar couldn't possibly have been in the building over fifteen minutes.

The point of a safe, of course, is that most burglars *aren't* expert safe men, which Sam didn't seem to have thought of.

"Fire safety," he replied. "It's got some real high kind of fire rating, as long as the door is closed, and I do usually keep it closed. I didn't bother with it today on account of I'm here anyway." He added, thoughtfully, "Anyhow, I suspect the only thing in it that would burn is the will."

"Will?" I asked.

"Yeah, you know, you can't keep wills in a safe-deposit box."

That is perfectly true, and it's a serious mistake a lot of people make. If you keep wills in a safe-deposit box, they become inaccessible as soon as the bank learns about a death, and banks are usually very quick to learn about deaths. They have people whose job it is to do nothing but read obituary columns. And once a death has been reported, it takes a court order—and the presence of somebody from the IRS, quite often—to get that lockbox open.

But a will? Whose will? I'd been told not two hours before that both Sam's and Margali's wills were at the moment in Margali's safe.

Sam didn't seem to be missing anything; at least if he was he hadn't noticed it. Reopening the safe, he dredged out a brown manila envelope. "Margali's will," he explained. "She's got mine and I've got hers. The lawyers, they said that was the best way to do it. See? Not in a lockbox."

"I should think storing it with the lawyers would be the best way to do it," I said.

"Well, now, I just don't like to store stuff with lawyers."

Sam thrust the manila envelope—which was indeed the appropriate size and shape for a will—back into the safe. "You make yourself at home, now," he said. "I won't be back in here for a long time. Sleep all you want to, or if you want a look at my scrapbooks—"

"Scrapbooks?"

"Yeah, scrapbooks, photograph albums, that sort of thing." He gestured expansively toward a wall of shelving piled high with assorted souvenir books. "You might want to look at some of them. Back when Marjorie was acting, I kept all sorts of things."

"Oh, how interesting," I said. "Maybe later, but right now I think I'll just rest."

I did indeed think so. The adrenaline generated by the discovery of the altered cans had worn off, and my now-customary lethargy was creeping over me. I really ought to call Captain Millner. I had an attempted murder going on. I really ought to make an official report of it.

But Susan had the matter under control. I'd call Captain Millner later.

Later today . . . or maybe tomorrow would be soon enough. . . .

No. I don't normally go to sleep and leave a murderer stalking his victim.

But I didn't, now, think there *was* a murderer.

Or rather, I didn't think Margali Bowman was the intended victim.

Yes, the Diet Coke cans contained a substance never put there by the Coca-Cola Bottling Company. I was quite sure of that; I wasn't holding off for a laboratory analysis this time.

But I'd seen—and Susan also had seen—the satisfied smirk on Margali's face as she peered around to see Susan, Fara, and me examining the cans. She knew what was going on. She knew what was in those cans.

Yes. She'd seemed terrified, this morning, on the patio. But she was an actress. And that was what I had let myself forget.

If there was an intended murderer, it was Margali, I thought then.

And the only intended victim—so far—had been me. And I wasn't even sure of that. Because what I wasn't sure of, until we did get the lab analyses, was how much poison was in any of the cans. Margali most likely wasn't trying to poison anybody—at least not fatally. She'd certainly have made sure of that with the first dose, the one she took herself.

Which didn't necessarily mean she wouldn't do it. She could wind up like the woman who kept getting in fights with her husband, and each time she'd run off to a motel, put on her most elaborate makeup and prettiest nightie, do her hair to make it look its best, take a deliberate OD, and then make sure her husband found it out in time to save her life. Until the day that she called a neighbor and asked her to call hubbie—at once—and tell him the car was at the Holiday Inn and he knew where he'd find *her*.

The neighbor, who was new in town, talked it over with *her* husband and decided not to get involved.

By the time a cleaning woman found her, three days later, the prettiest nightgown and the nicest hairdo and the most careful makeup in the world didn't do her a bit of good.

It was winter. The heat was turned up high. Her face, dusky blue, was swollen with the body fluids that were draining from her mouth and nose and ears, and no amount of perfume could mask the stench in the room.

No, it wasn't suicide. It was a particularly nasty attempt at extortion that had gone wrong. Since there was no insurance involved, we let it go as accidental death for her children's sake.

If Margali's poison killed anybody, it would be that kind of accident. She wouldn't mean to.

But the victim would still be just as dead. As I might be right now, if I'd finished that Diet Coke she gave me this morning, and nobody would have been more surprised and grief-stricken than Margali.

But she wouldn't do anything else now. She'd allow time for there to be a lot of commotion over the cans and whatever they contained, and she would be very surprised when I slapped her with a search warrant and went and found the syringe, the needle, the solder and soldering iron, and took possession of the fire salts.

But tomorrow—after her birthday—would be quite soon enough for that. Susan and I would take care of it then. And this time, there might really be enough to get Margali Bowman/Marjorie Lang committed, at least for a while. No, she'd never deliberately harm anybody. Not me, not my unborn baby. But if her attempts to get attention were likely to turn into even accidental murder, then it was no longer safe for her to be on the streets.

So we'd take care of it tomorrow. For now I'd just have a little nap. I wasn't frightened, now. I wasn't even—really—mad at her. Because I knew for sure that she wasn't deliberately trying to harm me; it was just that she'd slipped over that line dividing sanity from insanity, and maybe—maybe—Susan could pull her back onto the right side of the line again.

And then the only problem would be why in the world she had four, or however many it was, wills.

· 6 ·

I woke suddenly, with no memory whatever of having dozed off, and for a moment I wondered what had wakened me. Something certainly had; my heart was pounding as it never does when I wake normally. No, something had startled me as I slept and now, awake, I couldn't remember what it had been.

Then I heard it again—a stealthy footfall that caught my attention as a normal step probably wouldn't have.

Something slithered—a book that had been lying flat, pulled out from under other books?

Someone said, very softly, "Damn!"

Papers rustled and stopped rustling. A moment's silence. Then someone was walking quietly through the darkened room toward the bed on which I was lying.

"Hey, Deb, you awake?"

My eyes were open. But Sam's miniblinds were quite effective. I could see that someone tall and lean was standing beside the bed, but that was all I could make out.

All right. Time for logic. Tall. Lean. Male voice. Unconvincing male voice. It had finished changing—it was grown-up—but there was something about it that still didn't sound quite male. Or, maybe, it wasn't so much not quite male as it was not quite normal. In some way, not quite human.

"Jimmy?" I said.

He laughed softly. "Okay. I didn't know whether to turn on the lights or not. I didn't want to scare you."

He stepped back and reached for the light switch, and I automatically threw one arm over my eyes and then, cautiously, sat up, blinking. "I was asleep," I told him. "Until you came in."

He laughed again. Jimmy Messick laughed a lot; he laughed as much as his sister shook her head. The laughter never sounded quite real. It didn't this time, as he sat down beside me on the plaid bedspread.

"You want to look at pictures?" he asked.

"Not especially."

That was rude of me. I don't like to be rude, even to people I don't like, and I definitely did not like Jimmy Messick. "What kind of pictures?" I mumbled.

My mouth felt glued shut. Without waiting for Jimmy's answer, I scrambled off the bed and tottered to the adjacent bathroom, shutting the door behind me. A paper-cup holder was on the wall on one side of the long mirror, and I got a drink of water and washed my face, shamelessly using Sam Lang's washcloth and soap and reflecting as I did so that I wasn't at all sure I'd have been willing to use Margali's. Not now. There was a time when I would have.

When I came out Jimmy Messick was sitting exactly where I had left him, on the side of the bed. "Scrapbooks," he said. "Clippings. You know."

"Huh?"

"You asked what kind of pictures. I'm telling you. Scrapbooks. Clippings. That kind of pictures." His tone would have been no more than a civil reminder to someone who'd lost track of a conversation, except for that overtone of mockery that was never absent.

This time he didn't wait for me to answer. He opened the cover of a dusty red scrapbook. "That's my mother," he told me. "Gorgeous, wasn't she?"

"Beautiful," I agreed. It wasn't a lie. This picture must have been forty or more years old. It was black and white, not color, but the thick and glossy paper hadn't begun to yellow, and although it was impossible to see the red of her hair, its sheen was obvious. She was wearing some kind of slinky, formfitting gown, and over that she held some kind of white fur wrap at arm's length away from her body; she seemed almost a brilliant butterfly with an exotic beaded thorax and thick white wings.

The cellophane tape that held the clipping to the page was yellow, cracking, its peeling edges grimy and tacky to my fingers.

He turned a page. How old *were* these pictures? Margali, in some kind of playsuit with cuffed legs that went to mid-thigh, was stretched out seductively along the wing of a bomber, in a World War II pinup pose.

Following was a wedding picture—a photograph, this time, rather than a clipping—but it, too, was anchored with peeling yellow cellophane tape.

It wouldn't have been Jimmy's scrapbook; he wasn't old enough, and anyway this was Sam's bedroom—yes, and that was Sam in the photograph, Sam incredibly young, slim, handsome—Sam in uniform, Sam and Margali laughing, Margali with her right hand slightly lifting the skirts of a traditional wedding gown as she and Sam rushed beneath an arch of crossed swords. Crossed sabers? Had Sam been a West Pointer?

I asked, and Jimmy nodded. "Money'll buy a lot," he said.

"Money won't buy West Point," I told him.

He shrugged. "It helps. Even there, it helps."

I shook my head. Jimmy was flipping pages again. I got glimpses: "Storybook Marriage Turns Sour?—Margali Caught in Royal Love Nest—"

All clippings, now. All clippings.

If Sam was an officer, he'd have been at the front. Maybe? Or at the Pentagon, or was it the Pentagon then? I'm no historian, and I was a baby while these things were going on. I was a baby, and Jimmy Messick wasn't born.

Whose scrapbook? Was Sam keeping it even then?

I was more and more curious. All right, I am nosy. I have never denied that. I asked.

"Sam's mother kept it, while Sam was overseas. Overseas. He was in London. Some kind of attaché. I guess it wasn't a perfect job—they were having bombs and stuff in London—but I've always had the idea it was sort of a cushy job. But anyhow Sam's mother kept the scrapbook. And then she sent it to Sam. Sweet of her, wasn't it? Real sweet?" Jimmy laughed. "But believe it or not, he wasn't interested. It was Margali who got the divorce."

For a moment Jimmy stopped turning pages, so that I could see a picture—another photograph, this time—of Margali by the side of a darkly handsome man in Western dress topped by an elaborate burnoose. "Ali Hassan," Jimmy said. "*Prince* Ali Hassan." He laughed. "Prince. Yeah, sure. Hollywood loved princes. So a lot of people obliged. Ali Hassan was a prince like Michael Romanoff was a prince."

"Who?"

"Michael Romanoff." Jimmy glanced at me. "You never heard of Michael Romanoff? Romanoff's? That restaurant, you know?"

I didn't know. But I sat and tried to look as if I did, and Jimmy went on. "But Ali Hassan had money. No crown, but Lord, did he ever have money. I don't know where he got it—oil, I know that, but I don't know how he got title to the land the oil was under. He had it, that's all I know. What he didn't have was good sense."

"Oh?"

"From what I've heard, he was the kind of guy that if he'd had any brains, he'd have taken them out and played with them. Dumb, handsome, and rich. He and Margali were made for each other. They might even have stayed married two or three years, except—"

He turned the next page and unfolded a newspaper clipping, the upper half of a front page. The screamer headline— "Margali Bowman Escapes Injury!" And the subhead—"Millionaire Playboy Dies in Mystery Crash!" Minor headlines, barely above the fold, gave the world news: Roosevelt was announcing new rationing; there'd been big battles in the Pacific; ships were missing in the North Atlantic.

"It wasn't what you'd really want to call a mystery crash," Jimmy told me. "What happened was, she got drunk and climbed a tree in his Jag. He was passed out. The tree was on his side of the car."

"They had Jaguars then?"

"Whatever. Maybe it was a Jag, maybe it was a Stutz Bearcat, what the hell difference does it make? They were both drunk as pissants and he got dead and she didn't. And my dear sweet sister was born seven months later. Margali's kinda got a genius for having posthumous babies, wouldn't you say? Or would you?"

"Well, I—"

Jimmy was standing up, walking back toward the shelf. He yanked another scrapbook out and returned the first carelessly to the top of the teetering heap. "This is Sunny Messick," he announced, flopping down beside me again.

Another gala wedding scene. Another traditional wedding gown. This time the groom was wearing a tuxedo; there was no arch of sabers. Margali looked flushed and excited. She also looked a little older. Not a lot older. Just a little.

This was the first color picture, and the colors weren't quite true. I wasn't sure, in fact, whether it was real color photography, or whether the photo had been hand-tinted, as pictures so often were in the forties and fifties.

Jimmy's fingertips brushed the faces. "My mother's got blue eyes," he told me.

"I know that."

"Sure you know that. How long have you known my mother?"

"About thirty years, why?"

"You knew her before I was born."

"That's right. A long time before you were born. Five years, to be exact."

"You ever meet Sunny Messick?"

"No, I didn't."

Once again Jimmy's fingertips brushed the faces. "He had blue eyes, too."

According to the pictures, that was perfectly true. Sunny Messick, even in his wedding photograph, had a shock of tousled blond hair, blue eyes crinkled with laugh lines, square mechanic's hands with ground-in oil that hadn't quite all come out even for this extraordinary occasion. He looked likable, easygoing—but in my mind I could hear Fara's voice: *I hated him . . . he was always trying to feel me up. . . .*

"You hear me?" Jimmy repeated into my ear. "I said, he had blue eyes, too."

"So?"

"So?" Jimmy looked full into my face. "So what does that make me?"

"I don't know, what *does* that make you? I'm sorry, I don't know what you're talking about."

"Oh, hell, Deb Ralston, what the hell did they teach you in school about genetics?"

I couldn't remember having ever studied anything in school about genetics. I said so, and I told him that I hadn't the faintest idea what he was getting at.

"I'll tell you what I'm getting at! I'll tell you what the hell it makes me! It makes me a bastard, that's what. You ever hear of two blue-eyed people having a brown-eyed kid? Did you? You damn well didn't, and the reason you didn't is because it can't be done."

Even I, with my less-than-limited knowledge of genetics, knew that. But—"Your eyes aren't brown. They're green."

"Oh, hell, Deb, I've got brown eyes. Sometimes they look green, that's all."

"Brown eyes don't look green. Hazel eyes look green sometimes and sometimes in some lights they look brown. I've got hazel eyes and my parents both have blue eyes and they're damn sure my very own parents."

Jimmy laughed harshly. "Have it your way. But I'm not any kin to Sunny Messick. Even my mother told me that."

"Then she must have told you who you are kin to."

"She did. Oh, she did tell me that."

"You want to tell me?"

"You out of your mind?"

"Then what are you leading up to?" I asked warily. Why did everybody in this nut ward of a house want to come sneaking in where I was trying to sleep to tell me things that were none of my business?

"It sure was lucky for Margali that Sunny died when he did. She never would have been able to convince him I was his, and from what they tell me, Sunny, now, Sunny had a temper that was out of this world. Oh, he believed it then. That's why they were kissing all over the racetrack." He was turning pages again, letting me see glimpses of Margali's life as the gossip columnists, the fanzines, had seen it. "But after I was born— he'd have known then. So wasn't it lucky for Margali Bowman that Sunny Messick died when he did? 'Course Fara, she really is Ali Hassan's kid; all you got to do is look at her to know that—lucky for her, with all that money—but before she was born, you s'pose Margali knew for sure? You s'pose Margali really knew?"

He snapped the scrapbook closed, suddenly, and looked at me with a kind of indecent triumph. "So poor ol' Ali Hassan, who was about as much a prince as I am, but he had that Arab pride, you know, died before his kid was born; and poor ol' Sunny Messick died before his kid was born—and one was and one wasn't—and wasn't that lucky for Margali? Wasn't it really lucky?"

"Jimmy, even if Margali could have staged the wreck that killed Ali Hassan, Sunny Messick died on a racetrack. There was no way in the world Margali could have had anything to do with that."

"You sure? You real sure about that?" Jimmy Messick leaned forward. "One of his pit crew died about six weeks later. Seems the poor fellow was a photography nut—did his own developing and all that. And one morning he put cyanide crystals he used back in the darkroom into his coffee cup in mistake for sugar. Poor fellow. Nobody ever could figure out how it happened. He was alone at the time. And he sure was a Margali Bowman fan. Had a lot of pictures of her all over the place. Oh, it was a sure-enough accident. He kept the cyanide crystals in an old peanut butter jar in the darkroom and he kept the sugar in an old pea-nut butter jar in the kitchen and somehow he got the two switched around. Funny how he did that, wasn't it? You s'pose he was drunk when he did it? Or you s'pose he had help? Just a little bit of help? 'Course there's no telling who helped him. His bed was all made up when they found him. So he got up in the morning and made his bed before he got his coffee—smart of him, wasn't it?"

"Jimmy, are you accusing your mother of murdering three people?"

"Now, would I do a thing like that to my own mother? She's had five husbands. Sam was her first. He's also her fifth and seventh, but I only counted him once. She's had seven wed-dings. Two of 'em are dead—no, make that three. Or—no, by golly, I do believe it must be four now. Let's see, there was that singer, what's-his-name, I forget. I could look it up, but why bother? They called him an up-and-coming star. He was the one after Ali Hassan, I think—no, I'm not sure. Was he? I guess. That was before my time. He never did do much of anything after he married Margali—sat around and soaked up that good ol' California sunshine. Then Margali divorced him and he shot himself, poor fellow. And Cal, he was the last one except for Sam, he was some kind of bit player or something; she married Cal when I was about fifteen."

"I thought she was married to Sam then," I interrupted. "She and Sam got married when you were about three, didn't they?"

"Yeah. Then they got unmarried. Then she got married to Cal. Then she got unmarried to Cal. Then she got married to Sam again. I thought you knew about that."

"No, I didn't know—" I paused. Why didn't I know? I should have known. Obviously I knew; I knew how many times Margali had been married and that meant that in some part of my mind I had to know about this set of divorces and remarriages.

Oh well, I thought. Clearly my mind was trying to play tricks on me. Probably I had heard about Cal, but I'd definitely never met him, and I'd just gotten tangled up as to exactly when he came in. No wonder—I suspect you'd need a computer to keep track of all Margali's comings and goings in the matter of matrimony.

Jimmy was still talking about Cal and Margali; clearly Cal had made a bigger impression on his memory than on mine. Which made sense, I suppose.

"He was about twenty-nine. She was in her fifties or sixties or something then. They stayed married about a week. Margali threw him out. And then she spent about three days throwing away his things. Wouldn't let the maids do it. Wanted to do it herself. I remember she threw a bottle of Aramis through a plate glass window and one of the neighbors called the cops." He chuckled. "Poor Cal, he died of AIDS a couple of months ago. Never did get to be anything more than a bit player. See, he thought Margali would be his leg up. He figured she'd be delighted with somebody nice-looking to squire her around. It was his bad luck he picked a broad that wanted more than courtly attention. Now, Sam, he's careful. Sam is real careful— but then Margali wants to keep Sam, so she just pays the gardeners extra on the sly, that sort of thing. She didn't care the first time. But then the first time she didn't have to pay for it, and she knew if she lost Sam, she could always replace him. Now—uh-uh."

I shouldn't have been listening to this. But in a sick sort of way, it was too fascinating to shut off.

"Like I said, Margali wants to keep Sam. He's rich. He's fairly presentable, when he's not playing like he's Lyndon Johnson, that is. What I can't figure out is, how come Sam hasn't gotten rid of *her*. It must be pity. I mean, she's not fooling him; he knows about the gardeners and all, but he—hey, Sam; he's— fastidious, you know? Who'd want to sleep now with a pig like Margali? Not Sam. But I guess he's sorry for her. He loved her once. Can you believe it? He really did love her once."

Jimmy sat silently beside me, the scrapbook closed and his hands, still for the first time since I'd met him, resting on it, while the word "love" hung in the air between us like some tawdry, tarnished bit of grab bag finery.

Suddenly he said, "I'm an actor too, you know."

"Fara said something about that," I hedged. "I can't imagine why I haven't heard of any of your films. I—uh—must not pay enough attention to—"

"You just don't move in the right circles. 'Course my mother, she doesn't know; figures from what I've told her they're great big feature films; can't figure out why they never come to Fort

Worth or Dallas; can't figure out why I never have gotten tapes of them she can show on the VCR. I've got the tapes, all right, but if she saw them, she'd shit little green apples."

"Oh, that kind of actor."

"Yeah. I'm real good at it."

"That's nice," I said feebly, wishing we could get off this topic at once.

"My thing's twelve inches long," Jimmy announced. "You want to see it?"

"No, thanks. Uh—how'd you convince your mother the films were—"

"It was real easy. I didn't ask her for money for two months. Two *whole* months. And she knows how much I spend in two months."

"Oh, blue movies make that much?"

"Some do. 'Specially if you've got a sister who doesn't want the movies distributed." He laughed again. "A sister with a whole lot of money. You know what? My mother's real proud of me. Sometimes, anyway. That's a joke, isn't it? That's a real good joke. Why aren't you laughing? I think it's real funny, don't you?"

He sat still for a moment. Then he snapped the scrapbook closed, thrust it under another scrapbook, and sat down beside me again.

"Jimmy," I asked, on the track of something too ephemeral to have finished forming in my mind, "if Fara died, who'd get her money? Her husband? The girls?"

"Uh-uh. It all goes back to ol' Hassan's family, unless Fara has a boy; then he gets it all. Them Arabs, they don't even think women have souls. Why?"

I shook my head. I didn't know why. Not yet. Only—if Margali spiked that Diet Coke and it wasn't meant for me, who was it meant for? Could it have been meant for Fara?

Had Margali ever noticed Fara had quit drinking Cokes entirely?

Did Margali understand how Ali Hassan's estate was tied up? (And was Jimmy right—or telling the truth—to begin with?)

Was Margali money-hungry enough to kill her daughter for oil wealth she thought she might inherit?

"Cat got your tongue?" Jimmy asked.

I jumped. Then, as much to see his reaction as to get his answer, I asked, "There's not a TV show, is there?"

Jimmy shook his head. "She wants there to be a TV show. So there must be one, because she wants there to be one. She's the has-been mother of a never-was son. The old bat's gaga, can't you tell that? Why do you care anyway?"

My mother's crazy and nobody but me even seems to care— Fara had put it more gently.

But she'd said the same thing, or part of the same thing. Could Jimmy be right, was there even an outside possibility that Margali had somehow contrived the death of Ali Hassan, of Sunny Messick, or that unknown pit crew member? Because if it was true—what did Sam drink?

Did Sam ever drink Diet Cokes?

Had anything besides Diet Cokes been doctored?

What did *Sam's* will say?

I didn't get a chance to go on wondering, or to ask Jimmy any questions that might have cleared any of this up in my mind— such as, Why in the world are you telling me all this?—because down the hall, someone was screaming.

A book I read once said that the biggest difference between cops and ordinary people is that ordinary people run away from trouble, but cops run toward it. In a way that's true, but then on the other hand, you've always got the problem of rubber-neckers, people who can't possibly help, but come to gawk and get in the way. There were already four of the house servants clustered in the hall—I guess they must have been cleaning nearby—and I had to elbow my way through them to get into Margali's room.

Inside was complete pandemonium. The white fur coverlet, spread neatly over the bed two hours ago, now trailed onto the floor, and the bookcase full of paperback romances and fashion magazines was pulled out from the wall.

But I didn't notice that at first. The first thing I saw was a struggling mass of humanity on the floor—Margali, on top of Susan; Margali, with her hands around Susan's throat; Susan trying not very successfully to shove her off.

Margali, incongruously, was not screaming, "I'm going to kill you!" No, she was screaming, "I'll cut you out of my will!"

Not, you understand, that I took the time to examine the scene, or listen closely. I just caught Margali by her flying hair and none too gently pulled her head back.

Not too roughly, either, of course. A good yank on the hair from behind can snap a neck as easily as a hangman's noose. I didn't want to kill Margali; I just wanted to get her off Susan.

There was, however, a slight problem. I am five feet two. Margali was five feet seven. I was pregnant and, like virtually every pregnant woman, my strongest instinct was to protect my baby. Margali was in her seventies at least, but she was fighting with the strength and ruthlessness of the drunk and the mad—because she was surely both. Most likely she could demolish both Susan and me even without the problem of my pregnancy, and still come out hunting someone else to fight.

I couldn't defeat her. So I had to out-think her. And fortunately, drunks are often very easily distracted.

Pulling her hair had caught her attention. By now I had let go and she wasn't sure what it was she'd noticed. She was looking at me now, but she still had her hands on Susan's throat. "Margali," I said earnestly, "you've got to help me. Somebody put my suitcase somewhere and I can't find it."

She stared at me. Her grasp on Susan's throat was slowly relaxing, and Susan hadn't been anywhere near stopping breathing anyway. "I don't know," Margali said vaguely. "Why would I know?"

"It's your house," I said, "and remember, you did let me take a nap in your lovely room. Could it be in here somewhere, do you think?"

Now her attention was wholly on me. She stared vaguely around the room. "Maybe—"

"Margali, please do come help me."

She began to stand, and Susan hastily rolled out from under and headed for the door, to croak a quick order to Darlene. Margali poked ineffectually around in the wreckage. "Not here," she said. "Maybe—"

Turning, she caught sight of the ravaged bookcase. She screamed and started toward it.

"Margali, what is it? What's wrong?" I clutched at her arm in feigned horror.

Maybe I am not a very good actress. But on the other hand, Margali was drunk. That helped.

"Debra! Burglars!" she shrieked.

"Burglars? What did they take?" I gasped, falling back, clutching her arm again, and fighting an overwhelming urge to burst out laughing.

"They're trying to poison me!" she wailed. "Look! Look, Debra, look!"

In totally unfeigned surprise, I dropped to my knees, peering behind the bookcase.

A syringe. A large hypodermic. A complete electric soldering-iron kit, so new it still had the Sears price tag on it. Exactly what I had surmised had been used.

"What are they trying to poison you with, Margali?" I asked, still on my knees behind the bookcase.

"They put it in the Cokes. It was in the Cokes, wasn't it?

Because I drank a Coke and I got sick and you drank a Coke and you got sick. So it was in the Cokes. Diet Cokes, I mean; I don't drink plain Cokes. In my business one can't afford to be fat. And you found out—I knew you found out when you made Fara take all the Diet Cokes away. They're trying to poison—"

"But Margali, there's nothing here—I mean, there's no poison. So even if this is what they used to put poison in the Cokes, where did they get the poison?"

I looked up expectantly, wondering whether she was going to lead me to the fire salts.

She did not lead me to the fire salts. She turned around, saw Darlene and Susan, saw the filled hypodermic syringe in Darlene's hand, and began to shriek again—"You're trying to poison me!"—shriek, and head purposefully toward Susan. I moved in to block, but by now Olead was in the room too. As a doctor he's only a beginner—he's just finishing his first semester of medical school—but he's a very large, very strong man. And he'd die before he'd let anybody harm Susan or me. She's the doctor who gave him back his sanity, and I seem to have kept him from getting executed for murder. So he caught Margali from behind and held her while Susan pushed the cheerful polka-dotted puffed sleeve up the flabby blue-veined arm, and Darlene gave her the injection.

Olead continued to hold Margali as she slowly went limp in his hands. He lifted her then and stood holding her as Darlene hastily straightened up the bed, and then he placed her on it.

"She definitely does not," Susan observed, "have osteoporosis."

I laughed then. I couldn't help it.

"And that's the end of this party," said Harry from the doorway, as Darlene, carrying the now-empty syringe, slipped past him.

"Oh, no," Susan replied in almost her normal voice, briskly straightening her embroidered blue chambray shirt as she spoke. "She'll be out about two hours. When she wakes up, she'll be perfectly calm for a while. And of course dear Margali's birthday party must go on." She grimaced.

"And I want to be a psychiatrist?" Olead remarked, gazing at the supine figure on the bed. "Did I ever get like that, Susan?"

"Not exactly." Susan, poking around in the debris on the floor, had located a white plastic grocery bag. I wondered what she intended to do with it.

"How not exactly?"

"I've never seen you drunk."

"Don't hold your breath waiting to see me drunk."

Susan was advancing on the paraphernalia behind the book-case, and I quite suddenly snapped out of my near-trance. "Leave that alone!" I yelled.

Susan, Olead, and my husband Harry, who was still standing in the doorway, all turned to stare at me.

"Leave what alone?" Susan asked.

"That! Susan Braun, I could wring your neck! I know she's your patient, but it's my crime scene, and—"

"Your what?" Olead demanded, fairly reasonably I suppose in retrospect.

"I told you we'd get a search warrant tomorrow and go at it right, but no, you had to—"

"Do you think she would have been any calmer tomorrow?" Susan interrupted.

"No, but we'd have been legal, and—"

"Sure, we'd have been legal, but in the meantime—"

"You may very well have destroyed the evidentiary value of—"

"The hell with the evidentiary value! Suppose somebody else had been poisoned in the meantime?"

"Poisoned?" Harry asked. "What are you—"

"Suppose someone had died!" Susan raged on. "Then what use would your evidentiary value be to—"

"Susan, we do not have the legal right to search anything without a—"

"You don't, but I do. Look, Deb, you are a cop, okay?"

"You know damn well I'm a—"

"Will you please listen to me! You are a police officer. By law you do not have the legal right to search any location without a search warrant. But I am a doctor. Margali Bowman—Marjorie Lang—is my patient. I have been retained by her husband. My task is to keep her alive and try my best to make her well, or at least as close to well as possible under the circumstances. And that gives me the right—and for that matter the obligation—to search for anything that's involved in making her ill!"

"Then get the blasted booze out of the house, why don't you?" I sat down limply on the floor and then hastily rearranged myself; I had landed on top of a spike-heeled sandal that had been concealed by a taffeta skirt. "Look, Susan, I know what my rights and obligations and restrictions are. I do not know what your rights and obligations and restrictions are. That I admit. But look at it this way: We're assuming Margali put that stuff there. Sure, we have a basis for the assumption. But all the same, it is an assumption, not a fact. More than a guess, but a whole hell of a lot less than a fact. So suppose that assumption is wrong. Suppose Margali didn't put the stuff there herself. If she didn't, Susan, who did?"

Susan stared at me, silently.

"See what I mean?"

Susan sat down beside me in the middle of the floor. Despite my slightly malicious hope, she did not find the sandal's mate. "An hour ago you were sure Margali did it herself."

"I wasn't sure. I was making an educated guess. Susan, why'd you want to stir her up like that? You ought to have known she'd go off like a skyrocket. Why couldn't you have waited until she was out of the way, if you had to be in such a hurry to search without a warrant?"

Susan began to unpin one of her braids, which had worked loose in the struggle. Speaking around bobby pins, she said, "That was the whole idea, besides the fact that, as you know quite well, I can't get search warrants."

"I can. And what do you mean, 'that was the whole idea'?"

"I mean I thought she was out of the way, gawking at that horrible movie. I went back in there for a few minutes and she was sitting there weeping and moaning about how this film reminded her of poor dear Ali, and Fara was fluttering around her wiping poor dear Mumsy's face to keep her occupied—I expected her to break out the smelling salts any minute—and I figured it'd be a good time for me to slip in here and find the stuff and get it out of the way. She wouldn't have known until next time she wanted it. How was I s'posed to know the bloody film would break and she'd push Fara out of the way and come running in here?"

"Whether it broke or not, she could have come back in too soon. I mean, really, Susan, in this hogpen you could have searched for a week and not found anything."

"In that case I'd have stopped looking. But there are always the obvious places you look first—between the mattress and springs, behind the books in the bookcase, in the dresser drawer under the underwear, in the bottom of the laundry hamper, inside the clock—"

"Inside the clock?"

"Sure. I had a patient once who was still sky-high on some sort of drug three days after she'd been brought in. Couldn't figure out where in the world she was getting the stuff. She hadn't brought much from home—just a few clothes, some paperback books, and this pretty little china alarm clock she refused to be parted from. She said her dear dead sister had given it to her, or something like that. And finally one of the other patients tipped me off that she was using the clock as a stash. I checked and she was. Deb, you would be astonished at how many pills can fit inside a little bitty alarm clock."

"I'll have to remember that one."

"Can I say something?" Olead asked diffidently.

Susan and I both turned to stare at him; we'd forgotten he was there, and Harry in fact wasn't there now. "Sure, what is it, Olead?" I asked.

"Just, if somebody put something in something, it might have been Jimmy."

"What makes you say that?" Susan asked.

"You remember the day the Epsom salts got in the stew?"

"I remember very distinctly the day the Epsom salts got in the stew," Susan replied. "Was that Jimmy? I always thought it might have been; that was why I had him barred from the kitchen."

"You had me barred from the kitchen too."

"You were hanging around with Jimmy too much. Was the Ex-Lax at the Christmas party Jimmy too?"

"Yeah, but I didn't think that was funny. I tried to get rid of it."

"Okay," I said, "I gather that Jimmy has a history of—let's say—adding noxious substances to food?"

"Right."

"But it's a far cry from that to actual attempted murder," Susan pointed out.

"He might not have read the label," Olead suggested. "He might have just meant to be funny. He does things like that, and he's not very big on reading labels."

"That's true," Susan replied. "Thanks, Olead. We'll think about that one."

"I'm gone, now." He wasn't, quite, but he went out the door and shut it softly behind him.

So now Harry and Olead were both gone. Margali, despite

now being facedown on the bed, was snoring very loudly. And Susan and I were still sitting side by side on the floor in the midst of the debris.

"It's driving me crazy looking at this," I said finally. "Do you s'pose Margali'd get mad if we picked it up just a little?"

Susan shrugged. "If she does, she does. Personally I doubt she'll even notice. But it's driving me crazy too. We could call it therapeutic—it can't be good for her to be living in the middle of this. But what do we do about that?" She nodded toward the pulled-out bookcase. "Surely you don't want to leave it there?"

"You've found it and she knows you've found it. We might as well go on and collect it. But let me do it."

"Why?"

"Fingerprints."

"What good are fingerprints? If it's her stuff and she put it there—"

"If it's got her fingerprints on it, it doesn't mean jack. She could have handled it or somebody else could have put it in her hands when she was passed out drunk. But if it's got somebody else's fingerprints on it—or even more, if it's been wiped clean . . ."

After a moment Susan said, "Oh." She stood up. "I'll go see if I can find some trash bags and laundry baskets."

We began at opposite corners of the room and worked toward each other, mainly sitting or even crawling on the floor, periodically setting trash bags full of empty bottles and cans, torn magazines, empty candy, cookie, and cigarette wrappers, or clothes baskets full of dirty underwear and other clothing out into the hall, from which they were quietly removed.

"Yech," Susan said once.

"What is it?" I asked, trying to determine how many cards the deck I was collecting now contained. It seemed to be forty-three, unless I had lost count.

"She's spilled a drink. Or something. I can't tell. Yucko. Gross. This is sticky."

"You sound so professional, Doctor."

"I feel so professional. Oh, if the AMA could only see me now. This has ruined the carpet. Do you suppose this is where she was working? When she was fiddling with sodas, I mean."

"We may need to get samples and find out. But it would be awkward."

"To get samples? I thought with a search warrant—"

"Getting samples is no problem. I mean it would have been an awkward place for her to work. She could get at it so much more easily on the counter in the bathroom. If she did it at all, that is."

Susan straightened, rubbing the back of her neck and staring at me. "I started asking you a while ago and got sidetracked. You were sure. You were sure Margali did it and now you're not. Why not?"

"I'm not sure why not." I wasn't. There was that smirk on Margali's face as we got the cans out of the den; I was 100 percent certain, then and now, that Margali knew what was in those cans. But did she know because she'd put it there herself, or because she'd followed the same trail of evidence we'd followed and figured it out for herself? She was drunk, she was probably insane, but even her worst enemies had never called Margali Bowman stupid.

There was Jimmy's story, which would seem to point straight to Margali as a killer. But how much of Jimmy's story was true, and how much of it was Jimmy's imagination, or even Hollywood gossip?

"Deb?" Susan prompted.

"I don't know," I said again. "It's just—Susan, do you know how to use an electric soldering iron?"

"Me? No, why?"

"Because—how would Margali know how to use one?"

"She could learn. It ought to be easy enough. Don't they come with instructions?"

"Oh, sure, she could learn. But—think about it, Susan. Is something an option because it exists?"

"What—?"

"Something's only an option if you're aware of it. I thought of a soldering iron because I'm used to soldering irons. Harry's always soldering things. But you didn't think of soldering irons because you're never around them. Susan, would Margali think of a soldering iron to mend a hole in metal? Or wouldn't she more likely just try to cover it with a piece of tape or something like that?"

"I just thought of something," Susan said. "Just this minute. During the Vietnam War, the Vietcong used to use hypodermics to put battery acid in Cokes. Then the GIs would swill it down real quick—" She shook her head. "I was an intern. I got ahold of a few."

"How did they close up the holes?"

"That's just it. I don't know."

"Would Margali know?"

Susan shook her head. "How do I know what Margali would know? She'd know if she'd been in a movie about it."

"Come on, Susan," I said. "Margali was in movies during the Korean War. She was in movies during World War II. But I don't think she was doing much by the time of the Vietnam War. That was in the sixties."

"You said you were still visiting her in Hollywood then."

"Not the late sixties. The early sixties. I just don't think—I can't remember for sure. But I don't think she was in anything then. Anyhow, we're getting kind of far afield. The question is, would Margali know how to use a soldering iron to patch a hole in a can? And I don't think she would. I don't think she'd even think of it. Do you? Really?"

Susan glanced at the bed. She shook her head. "Damned if I know, Deb. Damned if I know."

Margali might not have done it, but we didn't know.

Jimmy might have done it, but we didn't know.

How dangerous—really—was Jimmy Messick, porno actor and practical joker?

How dangerous—really—was his mother?

□ 7 □

WE CONTINUED TO SIT side by side on the floor. Margali's bedroom was clean, or at least as clean as we were likely to get it. The carpet badly needed shampooing as well as vacuuming, and there were a lot of small things that I hadn't the slightest idea where to put. In desperation, I had thrust as many of them as I could into an otherwise totally empty bottom drawer, and heaped the rest on top of the low bookcase we'd now restored to its original position.

Finally I asked, "Susan, what *is* wrong with Margali?"

Susan almost sighed as she began to remove the bobby pins that had been anchoring her braids. "Let's say that her grasp on reality is tenuous at best."

"Yeah, but I mean what's wrong? Susan, I've known her, off and on, since I was in the sixth grade. She's not—this is not the Margali I know. She's always been scatty, sure, but not like this. What's happened to her? Has she got Alzheimer's or something? Or syphilis? I've read that can make people really strange."

"She does not have Alzheimer's or syphilitic paresis," Susan said precisely, unbraiding her hair as she spoke. "There's not the least reason to suspect Alzheimer's, and syphilitic paresis is extremely rare now. Anyway, lab tests will catch that. Syphilis, I mean, not Alzheimer's. She hasn't got it."

"But you ran the tests?"

"I ran the tests. Not that I suspected it, but just in case the question happened to come up. Anyway, her husband told me— Oh, hell, Deb, patient-doctor confidentiality, you know about that. Let's just say if one of my patients is likely to be infectious, I want to know it, okay?" She was now rebraiding her right braid.

"That's reasonable. Are you saying you can't tell me what's wrong with her?"

"Well, I shouldn't. But even besides that, you know how I hate labels."

"Does that mean you don't know?"

Susan half-laughed and started on the left braid. "You can say that if you want to. Deb, there are all kinds of labels, you know? Some of them are layman's labels that the medical profession doesn't even use anymore. Some of them are pretty precise now, such as some forms of manic-depressive syndrome we can control—not cure, but control—with lithium. Just like controlling diabetes with insulin. It's not cured; it's still there, creeping around doing all kinds of nasty organic damage, but it's controlled and the patient can lead a reasonably normal life within certain limits."

"Okay, is Margali manic-depressive?"

"Maybe. That may be part of it." She began to fish around on the floor with the hand that was not holding the braid.

"Here." I handed her a green rubber band that looked as if it had originally been used to wrap a newspaper. "Then why can't you just give her lithium?"

"That's the problem," Susan said. "Some forms of manic-depressive syndrome don't respond to lithium. And we don't know why and we don't know what the difference is. Is it the same disease and sometimes amenable to treatment and sometimes not? Or is it two or three or more different diseases with the same or similar surface symptoms? That's what we don't know. At least that's part of what we don't know. It's like schizophrenia."

She had my attention now. Susan's father, also a psychiatrist, many years ago had diagnosed a young teenager named James Olead Baker as schizophrenic. He'd treated him in all the normally accepted ways and Olead stayed schizophrenic. Then the old man died and Susan took over the Braun Clinic. Susan decided Olead, by then twenty-six, wasn't schizophrenic and probably never had been; she gave him vitamins, told him he was just fine, and turned him loose. And he was just fine.

"Schizophrenia is a lovely, lovely catchall," she was saying as she thrust bobby pins in at odd angles to semisecure the braids on top of her hair. "Sometimes you can treat it with psychotropic drugs. Sometimes you can treat it with megavitamins. Sometimes, but not very often, you can treat it with psychotherapy."

"That's where you lie on a couch and tell your dreams?"

"Not exactly. And sometimes you can't treat it with anything, and sometimes you get nice cases of spontaneous remission and then you go around for a while feeling like God and thinking whatever you were doing right then cured it, until the next time you try the same thing and fall on your ass. There are probably two dozen or more different ailments we're calling schizophrenia right now."

"Why?"

"Because we don't know what else to call them, I guess. But that's why I don't like labels."

"So is Margali schizophrenic?"

"How the hell should I know?"

"You're the shrink."

"Plastic surgeons think they're God. They can rebuild faces

and butts. They ought to try to rebuild souls. Then they'll find out real quick just how nothing a doctor is."

"Some psychiatrists think they're God," I argued.

"I know," Susan said gloomily. "Real dodo-brains, aren't they?"

"Dodo-brains?"

Susan looked embarrassed. "I have a six-year-old niece. Sometimes I pick up a little too much of her vocabulary."

I chuckled, and then asked, "But if you think she might be manic-depressive, can't you just *try* lithium? I mean, it can't do any harm, can it?"

"Oh, yes it can. Even when it's definitely needed, you have to watch it very closely. Look, Deb, I don't know what all is wrong with Margali. But one thing I do know is that she's an alcoholic. She drinks her breakfast and she drinks her lunch and she drinks her dinner and she drinks all day in between, and she's probably so far into negative balance on all the water-soluble vitamins that it's a wonder she can still walk. She's probably got scurvy and beriberi and you name it. If I ever get her into the hospital, the first thing I'm going to do is start her on an IV of all the water-soluble vitamins. That'll help a lot. After we get her blood chemistry back into something like working order, then I'll have a look at what else may be wrong. And there may well not be anything else." She looked over at the bed. "She'll be waking up pretty soon. We better get off this topic."

"Will she remember—" I gestured at the bookcase.

"I doubt it. If she does she'll probably think it was just a bad dream. Deb, you know I'm going to have to subpoena you to get a committal order."

"Okay."

"It won't cause you trouble with your friends?"

"Fara wants to get her into a hospital. The others aren't my friends anyway—but I think they all want her hospitalized."

Susan looked back at the bed. "Deb, I really think that her

fingerprints will be on that soldering iron and stuff. I really think she did it herself. I don't think anybody was trying to kill her."

"Neither do I. But I have to make sure."

Margali woke up then. She sat up, yawned, stretched, smiled beatifically at Susan and me, and said, "How nice of you to wait here for me to finish my little rest. But you didn't really have to do that. Debra, dear, get me something to drink, would you? There's some ginger ale there in the corner, I think, and, oh, Debra, dear, you might just add a smidgen of that Scotch to it, just enough to flavor it, you know."

Susan glanced enigmatically at me. I got up off the floor, washed my hands, got ice cubes out of the little bar refrigerator in the corner and dropped them into the glass that was sitting on top, poured in ginger ale, and added about a teaspoonful of Scotch.

"Oh, dear, just a little more than that," Margali chirruped.

I poured.

Susan was probably right. Nobody was trying to kill Margali except Margali, and she was doing a very good job of it. Ginger ale and Scotch, gaaa. We'd get her into the hospital. Susan would take the booze away from her and give her vitamins. And eventually we'd have Margali—the real Margali, with all her charms and imperfections—back.

That was what I thought. That was what Susan thought. That was probably what Fara thought.

We were, of course, all wrong.

But Margali was talked into a decent dress, and we ate a reasonably decent supper, and off we all went to the Blue Owl. Since it was a private showing, we could, of course, have gone right on in. But Margali had other ideas. When you go to the Blue Owl, you always go to the bookstore and browse. So we must all go to the bookstore and browse, and, of course, Margali was paying for all the books, because it was her party and this was part of the party.

I noticed that Sam looked a trifle annoyed at that, but he covered up quickly and echoed Margali's invitation.

Inside the bookstore everybody scattered. I didn't especially want a book—well, I did, but I wasn't going to let Margali buy me a book about pregnancy and childbirth after forty—so I stood by the counter and watched as everybody wandered back carrying books and magazines and looking more or less embarrassed. Susan, I noticed, had confined herself to a small volume of poetry, and Harry had a *Dragon Magazine* he'd take home and give to Hal.

When Margali opened her purse, inside I saw the damp, bulging manila envelope with a corner of the blue covering of the will sticking out.

Great, I thought, at least she—and it—would be safe for a while.

As I said, I was wrong. And now, four or so hours later, we knew just exactly how wrong I'd been.

Whether or not Margali had doctored the cans herself—whether or not Jimmy was right that Margali had killed or conspired to kill two of her husbands and a pit crew member—there was now no doubt at all that somebody had actually been trying to kill Margali Bowman. And whoever it was had succeeded—inside the Blue Owl, sometime between eight o'clock and midnight, with a police officer, namely me, sitting within spitting distance.

So who had done it?

It wasn't Harry or me. It wasn't my daughter or son-in-law. It certainly wasn't Susan or Darlene, because Susan's beeper had gone off twenty minutes after we entered the theater and when she left, she took Darlene with her. Nobody had come in from outside, because the projectionist had locked the theater to keep casual traffic out. This was SOP when someone rented the whole theater; the fire doors remained unlocked, of course, as per law, but they couldn't be opened from the outside.

So the possible suspects were Sam Lang, Jimmy Messick, Fara and Edward Johnson, Carl Hendricks (who had glumly returned to the house party), and Bob Campbell.

If Sam Lang wanted to get rid of Margali, all he had to do was get a divorce; that is easy enough in Texas even without stray gardeners who are paid extra for extraordinary services. Jimmy didn't have any reason to kill her; with her alive with her hands on Sam's checkbook, she was available to mooch from, but with her dead—with nothing of her own to leave him—he might, poor fellow, be thrown onto his own resources, which I suspected weren't very great. Fara and Edward had Fara's money, if money was a motive, which it couldn't be anyway; and although an alcoholic mother/mother-in-law might be an embarrassment to a team of self-styled evangelists, she couldn't be nearly as much of an embarrassment as a spectacular murder in the family.

What earthly reason would Sam Lang's business partner have for killing Sam Lang's wife? Even my imagination didn't extend that far.

Why would Margali's own attorney want to kill her? He couldn't be lying to cover up stealing from her, because she didn't have anything for him to steal. Of that I was sure. There was no imaginable reason for Fara to lie to me about that.

Or even, looking at a very long shot, what reason would the projectionist—a seventeen-year-old girl, working at the Blue Owl to save up money for college—have for killing a very old former actress she'd quite possibly never heard of before tonight?

If this were an Agatha Christie story, now, she'd turn out to be the long-lost daughter of the pit crew member, out to avenge the murder of her father—except, of course, that the pit crew member, if he'd ever existed and been murdered, had been dead something like twenty-six years, which made it entirely unlikely he'd have a seventeen-year-old daughter.

I wanted to go home and go to bed and eat chocolate candy and read Agatha Christie books. What's wonderful about reading paperback mysteries is that I don't have to do anything about the crimes in them. Everything is all miraculously solved, usually without the bother of such things as crime-scene crews and checking alibis.

Oh, hell, I thought, as the projectionist pulled out her ring of keys and raced up the stairs in response to a siren in the street outside, what difference does it make who had a motive? Look at it from a practical angle. Who had a weapon?

Two uniformed patrol officers—an Anglo male and a Chicana female—came down the stairs. Their name tags informed me they were Wilson and Gutierrez, respectively. Behind them came Captain Scott Millner.

He stopped long enough to send Wilson back up the stairs. The little projectionist came down without her keys. Presumably Wilson now had them.

Captain Millner is, by definition, my boss's boss. He is in charge of the entire Criminal Investigation Division of the Fort Worth Police Department, and Lieutenant Gary Hollister, a small foxy-looking man with curly red hair and a penchant for practical jokes, heads both the major case squad and the homicide squad. But in effect, most of the time Gary works with homicide and Millner personally supervises the major case squad.

I am part of the major case squad. But although we are perpetually overloaded—the optimistic plan under which the unit began, one person, one case, having long since vanished in the reality of big-city police work—we are not anywhere near as overloaded as homicide.

This means, of course, that the major case squad members often find themselves working homicide.

There's one more little rule. It is, unless there is some pressing reason otherwise, the first detective on the case is in charge of the case.

I looked at Millner. He is six feet two, with gray hair still cut in the same military style he wore in the Air Force thirty years ago. He is sixty-two years old and nobody, least of all Millner, has any intention of retiring him. He looks so much like a television cop that every now and then people are surprised to learn he really is a cop.

I went on looking at Millner. I suppose I must have looked rather guilty. I certainly felt guilty enough. After all, a—face it—prominent citizen of Fort Worth had just been murdered while I sat not twelve feet away, half-dozing and half-watching a Grade C movie, doing nothing whatever to prevent the killing—after the victim had told me somebody was trying to kill her.

"What happened, Ralston?" Millner asked me.

That meant he was at least mildly annoyed. When he's in a good mood, he calls me Deb. I told him what had happened.

He took his glasses off and rubbed the bridge of his nose. "So who did it?"

I told him I didn't know.

"What was the weapon?"

I told him I didn't know that, either.

"Shit," he said.

I thought so too.

I could hear the door upstairs opening again. You can't see the door from the lobby. The way the Blue Owl is laid out, you enter a street door beside a bookstore. I think the bookstore is owned by the same people who own the Blue Owl, because it never closes until after the last show at the Blue Owl starts. That way you can buy your ticket and then go wander around the bookstore until they're ready to let you into the theater.

Then you go out the street door of the bookstore and enter the street door of the theater, and you go straight back a dingy little hall, past a staircase that leads up to something—I think it's a storage area, because I've never seen anybody use the stairs. You go to the back of the hall and turn right and pass two little doors that lead, respectively, to the men's rest room, which I've never been in (I would say, "of course," but the fact is that in the course of my work, I've had to be in quite a few men's rest rooms) and the women's rest room, which contains a little anteroom that sometimes has a mirror and sometimes doesn't, depending on whether anybody's stolen it lately, and one stall containing a toilet that usually flushes and a sink that usually drains.

After you pass both rest rooms, you turn right again and go down a narrow staircase that leads, in case you're lost by now, back toward the front of the building. You get off the staircase and turn right again and there is the lobby, where you buy tickets, soda pop, herbal tea, popcorn, homemade cookies, and sometimes Blue Owl T-shirts, depending on whether or not there are any right then.

I think it's a sort of a marginal operation, but they get very good movies and I like to go there—usually. When it hasn't been rented for the night by Margali Bowman.

But obviously you can't see the street door from the lobby. You also can't hear it, unless the theater is awfully quiet.

Right now the theater was awfully quiet; Fara was the only one crying and she, of course, was crying quietly. So we could hear the door open, and close, and then we could hear several people walking. They all came in at once, or as at once as they could on that narrow staircase: Doctor Andrew Habib, pathologist, deputy medical examiner; Bob Castle and Irene Loukas, identification technicians, which, of course, also means crime-scene technicians; Gil Sanchez, medical examiner's investigator.

We now had a full house, except that I still seemed to be the only detective.

Doctor Habib, rocking back and forth on the balls of his feet—a habit that drives me absolutely dotty—looked at me expectantly and demanded, "Where is it? Did you get me a good one this time?"

"*She* is inside the theater," I told him. "And these people include her husband, her son, and her daughter."

"Oh, sorry," Habib said. "All right, lead on, Macduff." A moment later he said, "Damn, it's dark in here, isn't there any way to turn on some lights?"

I asked the projectionist—Mary Fillmore, she'd told me her name was—to turn up the house lights as high as they could go.

She did. We now had approximated the illumination of the average country and western bar. If you've ever been to a country and western bar, you know that is not very much illumination.

Habib, after the otherwise unnecessary legality of pronouncing Margali dead, waited until Irene had photographed the corpse and she and Bob were working methodically through the aisles before he began to examine the wound on the back of the neck. When he is examining a corpse, he pokes around with his fingers; since AIDS started getting into the news, he is a little more careful about wearing gloves, but he still doesn't always. He wasn't wearing them this time.

He also hums to himself. I don't mean hum as in sing with your mouth shut. I mean he says things like "hmmm" and "um-hum" and "huhhm" and "uh-*huh*." This is guaranteed to drive any detective working on the case into a state approximating that of shrieking frustration.

Sometimes he talks to himself. Occasionally he talks to his investigators, but right now the only investigator with him was Sanchez, and he was up front with Irene and Bob, crawling around on the floor with a flashlight. Occasionally—but very,

very rarely—he talks to the detectives, who have the primary need to know.

He would be absolutely insufferable if it was not for the fact that he is an extremely good pathologist. When he gives an opinion, you can treat it as a fact. When he gives a fact, you can treat it as carved in stone.

I was more than ready for him to give me a fact. Or an opinion. Or a lollipop. Or anything. In fact, I was just about ready to offer *him* a lollipop if he'd just quit that infernal *hmming* and tell me something.

Finally he looked up, blinked as if surprised to see me, and said, "Oh."

"I think *oh*. What've you got?"

He looked back at the wound. I hoped he wasn't going to start *hmming* again. Fortunately he didn't. He said, "It was something like an ice pick."

"An ice pick?" I repeated. An ice pick is not anything normally carried in a man's pocket or a woman's purse, nor is it an item usually found in a movie theater—even a small, marginally run movie theater—in the second half of the twentieth century in the urban United States.

In fact, I couldn't recall *seeing* an ice pick in the last two or three years.

"Not an ice pick," Dr. Habib said, rather irritably. "I said like an ice pick. Something between an ice pick and a stiletto. Diameter a little larger than an ice pick and a little smaller than a stiletto."

"Goodie," I said. "A stiletto's a knife, right? So what does it have to do with an ice pick?"

"It's sort of like a dagger but not exactly," he said helpfully.

I reminded myself that the dentist had threatened me with a complete set of dentures if I didn't quit grinding my teeth. "What does that mean?"

"Well, it's not exactly a knife. It was developed in northern

Italy around the last quarter of the sixteenth century, and it was sort of a weapon for noblemen. And their wives," he added. "Some of them were really richly ornamented, jeweled, all that sort of thing."

"What does that have to do with an ice pick?"

"It wasn't a cutting weapon. It had a triangular blade about, oh, a little over a quarter of an inch in diameter."

"Triangular?" I'd never seen a triangular blade, and found it a little hard to imagine.

"Yeah. So it was intended for stabbing, strictly for stabbing, not for cutting. And if it was twisted a little, it'd leave approximately a circular wound. This is a little more circular, more like what an ice pick would leave. Only an ice pick, you know, it's going to be less than a quarter of an inch at the base, generally, and a lot less at the point."

"So this weapon is more than less than a quarter of an inch in diameter and less than more than a quarter of an inch?"

"Is that what I said?" He sounded mildly surprised.

"That was what you said. Translated into English, you mean it's about a quarter of an inch in diameter?"

"Approximately."

"Maybe a heavy-duty ice pick?" I'd rather believe in a heavy-duty ice pick than a small, dainty, sixteenth-century Italian lady's stiletto.

"No, because it's less tapering than an ice pick and too thick, especially at the point. Besides that, an ice pick's too long. It would—well, with the angle of the wound, it would come out—"

"Never mind," I interrupted hastily, "there's no need to be too graphic. Just put it in your report. My stomach's delicate right now." Especially, I added mentally, with the rest room through the lobby and up a flight of stairs.

"Yeah, I noticed. I've been meaning to ask you about that. You sick or something?"

"Something." I've got to give the captain my glorious news, I thought. Dutch Van Flagg—the detective whose desk is nose to nose with mine—has already told me about three times that if he didn't know me better, he'd swear I was pregnant; Susan spotted it this weekend (if not sooner); and now Habib was starting to ask questions.

Fortunately he didn't pursue the matter. He just glanced back at the body. I decided to ask some more questions. "Could it be some sort of ranch tool?"

"I don't know anything about ranch tools. But I don't know what it would be. It's not an awl or a nail sink or anything like that."

"Those're carpentry tools anyway."

"Oh. Yeah. Well, it's not anything like that. Oh, and you're not going to find any visible blood on it," he added.

"I'm not? Why?"

"Well, because it was wiped. Look." He pointed with his flashlight, and I could see wrinkled cloth, smeared with reddish-brown. Habib was right. Whoever killed Margali had calmly stood behind her—in a theater with over half a dozen other people—and wiped the weapon on the white collar of the pretty tailored dress I'd talked her into wearing.

"When can I have it transported?" Habib asked. A body—any body except, perhaps, that of a member of his family—was "it" to him. I wasn't yet quite to the point of thinking of Margali Bowman as "it." I'd get there, probably, during the course of this investigation. But I wasn't there yet.

"Later," I said. "Let me get the family out of the lobby first."

But that posed another problem. Because like it or not, the family members were the chief—and for all practical purposes the only—suspects. Which meant that even if I decided to wait until tomorrow to ask questions, everybody would have to be searched before leaving. And I knew perfectly well I didn't have the ghost of a legality to stand on. Without appropriate warrants, I could not compel anybody, much less everybody, to agree to be searched, and probably whoever did it knew that quite well.

Even if they didn't, there was an attorney there to remind them. Of course, Bob Campbell was Margali's attorney, which meant that at least theoretically he ought to want her killer to be caught, but even so, he had to take note of legalities—and the lack thereof.

I told myself there was still a hope Millner might decide I was too deeply involved in this case, personally, to work it. It was a very forlorn hope, and one immediately dashed when I returned to the lobby. Millner took his glasses off, rubbed the bridge of his nose, put his glasses back on, and looked at me through them. "How long'll it take you to get reports ready?"

"Can't I wait and do them in the morning?" It was after 1:00 A.M. If I was very lucky, I might get to bed by three before getting back up at six, but if I had to do reports tonight, I might as well forget about sleep entirely. And telling myself I had slept half the weekend was absolutely fruitless. My body wasn't interested. It was demanding more rest now.

"Yeah, I guess that'll be soon enough. But be sure you let me know how you're planning to proceed."

He headed for the staircase, and I called after him, "Hey, tell that patrolman up there to come down here, would you?"

"Will do." He strolled on up the stairs, and after a moment Officer Wilson—I had forgotten his name until I saw it again—came down.

"May I have your attention, please?" I said. This was, I felt even then, a little silly, considering that besides me there were only ten people in the lobby—well, twelve, counting the patrol officers—and they all were looking at me. But how do you begin an accusation of matricide or spousal murder? Especially in front of a lot of people not currently suspects?

You don't, that's how. And I wasn't going to. Yet. Not exactly, anyhow.

"I may not need to spell out what's happened. We all know that Margali is dead." Fara moaned a little at this and grabbed Edward's arm. Edward didn't seem to notice her.

"What I hope you all realize," I went on, "is that it is almost one-hundred percent impossible for anyone to have come in from the outside. The projectionist"—I glanced at Mary Fillmore, who nodded—"locked the street door as soon as we came in. And that means that somebody in this room right now did it."

I've never made an announcement like that before. I've never had the need to. And I felt—just a little bit—like Hercule Poirot, using his little gray cells. Only Poirot would now be able to look at everyone's reaction, point his finger dramatically, and say, "*You* did it."

My little gray cells don't work like that. All I could see was a group of unhappy, uncomfortable people, all carefully not looking at each other. As for the appearance of guilt, well, in some situations a saint would look guilty. For example, I defy any female between the ages of fifteen and fifty to be able to walk alone across the lobby of a swanky hotel in her slinkiest evening gown and push the button for the elevator—while knowing the house detective, whom she doesn't know, is watching her every step from behind—without expecting, at least in some part of her mind, that at any moment someone is going to flash a badge and demand, "Now, girlie, where do you think you're going?" Never mind that it shouldn't be that way. My point is that it is.

So how much more guilty is someone going to expect to look, if he or she is one of a very few possible suspects in the murder of an old woman—even a not-so-innocent old woman? And, of course, the more guilty you expect to look, the more guilty you *do* look. The guilty fleeth where no man pursueth, but so, quite often, do the innocent.

"The only fair thing to do is search everybody for a weapon. Now, as Mr. Campbell there will certainly tell you if I don't, I have no legal right to do that. So if anybody objects to being searched, for any reason or no reason, you may certainly refuse, and I certainly won't draw any conclusions from that refusal. If not, I'll ask Officer Wilson to search all the men and Officer Gutierrez to search all the women. She can start with me, while Officer Wilson stays here with everybody else, and then I'll stay here while Officer Wilson escorts each of the men to and from the men's room and Officer Gutierrez escorts each of the women."

"Full body search?" Gutierrez demanded.

"Strip search, also women's handbags and so forth. Complete inventory."

In a strip search, the officer and the person being searched stand at arm's length from each other. The person being searched is instructed to remove each item of clothing one at a time and hand it to the officer, who checks all pockets, seams, and cuffs.

It is not amusing for either party. I expected Fara, for example, to refuse or to balk halfway through.

As it happened, she didn't. Neither did anyone else.

Need I say that no ice pick, no Italian stiletto, and nothing remotely resembling either was found. Outside of my own .38 service revolver, which I am required to have on me at all times, no weapon and nothing resembling a weapon was found either by Ray Wilson or Ramona Gutierrez, or by the two ident techs and the medical examiner's investigator who spent the rest of the night and half the next morning searching the theater.

It didn't help at all that during the searching, Susan returned, absolutely furious, to report that she and Darlene had spent half the night hunting a nonexistent address in an Arlington suburb where a patient of hers was supposed to be in severe difficulties, refusing to come out of a locked bathroom and divulge what he had swallowed until his psychiatrist had arrived.

She'd have gone straight home, she added, except that Margali shouldn't be returned home without Darlene there to take care of her. "What," she belatedly thought to ask, "is going on here anyway?"

"You can go home," I told her. "You can take Darlene home too. Margali doesn't need her or you. Not anymore."

Just then the transport crew came down the stairs, carrying a body bag on a gurney, and went briskly past us into the theater. Fara moaned softly again.

Susan looked at Fara. She looked at the door the crew had gone through. "Oh, shit," she said to me.

"I think 'Oh, shit'," I agreed.

Edward Johnson looked disapprovingly at both of us but said nothing.

□8□

"WELL, THAT WAS AN interesting experience to say the least," Harry told me. His tone was mildly malicious.

"So what was I supposed to do? Say some people have to be searched but others don't?"

"Oh, I'm not complaining, I'm just saying it was an interesting experience."

We were sitting in a booth in a little restaurant off Belknap. I forget what its name is right now; it's one of those places that gets a new name, management, and menu every three or four months.

I was the one who'd decided to stop. No, let me correct that. I was the one who asked to stop.

"It's nearly three A.M.," Harry told me.

"I'm hungry. And I certainly don't want to have to go home and cook. Anyway, I don't know if I have anything to cook."

"I thought you said you were tired."

"I am tired. But I'm hungrier than I am tired. And you know what happens when I get hungry."

That was when Harry turned the car into the parking lot of the next restaurant we passed, where I was now waiting for a tuna club sandwich with slaw and fries (the fries were extra) and a glass of milk. The glass of milk was to appease my conscience or the doctor or both; besides, Cokes are a little much at 3:00 A.M.

My sandwich duly arrived; so did Harry's Denver omelette. "I never can understand," Harry commented, "how you can leave a killing and immediately go out and eat."

"Don't soldiers eat in battles?"

"Only if they get the chance."

"Well then. Anyway, I'm hungry."

"I gathered that." Harry applied himself to the omelette, and then added, "It wasn't just getting searched that was novel. It was all those reporters too."

I didn't want to think about all those reporters. As we had headed for the door of the Blue Owl about half an hour earlier, we could see vaguely, through the glass, some people moving around outside. Rather late for anyone still to be on the sidewalk, I thought, and opened the door—and involuntarily closed my eyes against the barrage of strobes and floodlights that cut on as if the door had been a trip wire. And the questions—some reporters assumed we were part of the family, who had left earlier, but a few recognized me. "How's the investigation going? You ready to make an arrest yet? Who's he? Did he do it?"

"No comment at this time," I kept replying mechanically. "It's too early for suspects."

A few reporters chased us to the car, but even they quickly turned back; sooner or later the body could be moved, and then they could all get nice pictures of the covered stretcher to show all the viewers of the six o'clock news.

Two television vans, complete with ladders and microwave dishes, were parked in the street.

The ordinary Fort Worth murder—the ordinary murder in any modern city—doesn't merit this kind of coverage. Somebody had figured out who Margali was. Figured out, and spread the word.

"How am I ever going to clear this one?" I complained now to Harry. Clear—that's what you do to cases. Not solve. Solve is for detective stories—fiction. I solve puzzles; that is, sometimes I solve puzzles, when I have time to work them. I clear cases. Cleared by arrest. Only, I didn't know how I was going to clear this one.

"Danged if I know," Harry replied. "There's one detective in this family, and it's sure as hell not me."

Detective stories. They're what got me into this mess. When I was a kid, I read all the Nancy Drew and Hardy Boys books I could find. I also surreptitiously got mysteries out of my parents' room, out of my father's dresser. Some of them were hybrids, mystery/westerns, about a fabulous Texas Ranger named Jim Hatfield, the Lone Wolf, who very confusingly seemed sometimes to live in the nineteenth century and sometimes in the twentieth. I didn't understand fiction then; I assumed it must all be true.

I told all my friends I was going to grow up and be a Texas Ranger. When informed there weren't any women Rangers, I replied that I would be the first one.

There are, I think, women in the Rangers now. But I'm not one of them and don't, now, want to be. I like it just fine where I am—most of the time. Except when faced with what I, with all my reading, could only call a locked-room mystery.

How would Jim Hatfield go at this one? Or Henry Merrivale. He's the one who gets locked-room mysteries. I hadn't the faintest idea. I'm not Jim Hatfield. Or Henry Merrivale.

"I don't think Carl Hendricks ever got up from where he was sitting," I said, not sure whether I was talking to Harry or just thinking out loud.

"He didn't," Harry agreed. "He went to sleep. He was sitting in front of me to the left, and I could hear him snoring. Edward Johnson got up once, I think."

"But not to get popcorn," I said positively. Margali—or Sam— had paid for popcorn, cookies, and soda pop for all of us—as much as we wanted. But Edward hadn't availed himself of the invitation. He'd gone back to his seat empty-handed. I remembered that, remembered wondering where he'd gone, because he hadn't been gone long enough to go upstairs to the rest room. What I didn't remember was how long he might have stood in the aisle, directly behind Margali, before leaving or after returning and before sitting down. "And Sam got up twice," I added.

"Yeah. Once he came back with popcorn and a drink. I know because he spilled a little of the drink and swore. I don't know about the other time. I wasn't paying any attention."

"Neither was I," I agreed. "There just wasn't any reason to. Jimmy was back and forth about two dozen times, I did notice that."

"Yeah, he was back and forth about as many times as you were," Harry agreed.

"I couldn't help that," I said with as much dignity as I could muster. Pregnancy does seem to have a few built-in inconveniences.

"Maybe Jimmy couldn't help it either," Harry suggested. "I mean, look at it this way. If it takes him seven breakfasts and three lunches and five dinners and forty-nine snacks a day to stay skinny, what would happen if he ate like a human being? Maybe he'd dry up and blow away."

"That wouldn't be any loss to the world. Didn't Bob Campbell get up once or twice?"

"Once at least. I don't know about twice. And Fara got up at least once. Look, we all did, except Hendricks. Four hours and fifteen minutes of that bilge!"

"Harry, be nice; she's dead," I protested conventionally.

"Does that make bilge not bilge, just because one of the perpetrators of it got knocked off?"

"No, I guess not. If we could just remember who stopped behind Margali for any length of time—"

"Deb, everybody stopped behind Margali. Everyone had to, to adjust to the light change."

That was the problem. He was right. The Blue Owl is not laid out like most movie theaters, with center aisles and side aisles. It has one aisle only; you enter the theater and the aisle runs to your right; as you walk down it, the seating is in rows to your left. Margali had insisted on taking the outside seat on the second row from the back; she'd insisted on everyone else sitting in front of her. I supposed (but now I was the one being rude about the dead) that she wanted to make sure her captive audience stayed captive.

But the result was that everyone who left had to go past her. Everyone who returned had to pause, for a moment, beside or behind her, to readjust to the dim light.

So anybody in there, in theory, could have killed her except Carl Hendricks, who slept through the murder as well as through the movies.

In practice, my possible suspects were four: I was sure it wasn't Harry, Becky, Olead, or me. I had no earthly reason to suspect the little projectionist (although she had stepped briefly into the theater a time or two); and I refused to suspect Fara. Not because she was an old friend, but because she was the one who'd wanted me to be a member of the party.

If you were going to murder your mother—or anybody else for that matter—you wouldn't invite a police detective along on the trip. Would you? Well, not unless you wanted to lay a really good smoke screen.

I couldn't—really—eliminate Fara. But all the same, I had eliminated her. It was Sam Lang, or it was Edward Johnson, or it was Jimmy Messick, or it was Bob Campbell. One of those four.

Harry was silent, watching me. He's familiar with these blue hazes I fall into, a sort of self-hypnosis, while my brain in computer mode goes to work processing its earlier input. He knows, too, when the computer shuts off and it's safe to ask questions again. "No weapons at all?" he asked softly, and then glanced around. He's well aware of security. But we were safe; the one waitress left was at the other end of the building, well out of earshot.

Pushing the empty plate out of the way, I set my purse on the table and pulled out of it a wad of notebook pages, the inventory of possessions. "Sam had a pocketknife, a wallet containing cash and credit cards, a ring of keys, a checkbook, an appointment book and a pen and pencil set. Bob Campbell had a pocketknife, a wallet containing cash and credit cards, a ring of keys, a checkbook, an appointment book, and two fiber-tip pens, the eighty-nine-cent variety. Wilson kept both pocketknives—with the owners' permission, of course—but the chances of either of them being the weapon are exactly zero. Jimmy did not have a pocketknife; incidentally, neither did Olead. I guess they're not as popular among younger men."

"I expect they never got in the habit," Harry returned. "I mean, I would think that mental hospitals wouldn't usually—"

"Encourage pocketknives. You're undoubtedly right. Anyhow, Jimmy had a ballpoint pen, a wallet containing cash and credit cards, and a key ring. Edward had a pocket-size Bible, a wallet containing cash and credit cards, a pocket notebook, two plastic-tipped dime-store-quality pens, and a ring of keys. Fara," I said reluctantly, still not willing to consider her a suspect, "had nothing but clothes on her person. In her bag she had keys, a billfold containing cash, credit cards, a checkbook and a pen, a grocery-store-coupon caddy with a lot of coupons in it, a wad of Kleenex, a small hairbrush, and a rat-tail comb—aluminum. Gutierrez kept the comb, with Fara's permission. And the chances of it being the weapon are exactly zero. Are you going to finish that omelette?"

Harry looked at his plate. "No."

"Then can we go home? I'm tired."

Harry did not remind me of whose idea it had been to stop. That was nice of him.

Never mind about Sunday. I suppose it existed, but it never had a chance to feel like Sunday to me. I suppose Harry took Hal to church or else Hal got a ride; lately he's started going to this church clear over by the 820–121 split, and he's antsy about missing it. I even go with him, sometimes. I'm getting to kind of like it.

But I didn't go that morning. I went to the office and wrote reports—dictated them, actually, onto a tape recorder for a clerk to type later. I dodged reporters. I did not read the newspapers. I didn't want to read the newspapers.

I went back to the Blue Owl and tried to think where I'd be if I were an ice pick. That was my mother's standing order when one of us kids had lost something, and it was usually just as much of an exercise in futility as it was this time. I checked all the trash cans in case nobody else had, but of course I knew quite well they'd already been checked at least once, and more likely twice.

I went and talked to Fara and Edward (after church, of course), and that was another exercise in futility. Edward informed me that the ways of the Lord are mysterious, and he who lives by the sword shall die by the sword.

"In what way did Margali live by the sword?" I asked.

I won't try to remember his exact words. He was of the opinion that movies—especially Margali's movies—appealed to the lusts of the flesh and facilitated sinful behavior. He quoted Isaiah, something about daughters of Jerusalem who walked with mincing footsteps and veils and were going to be smitten with scabs, and I excused myself and left.

He might even in some ways be right. But did he have to be so prissy about it?

But anyway it had gotten to be four o'clock and all the records

I wanted to consult were probably locked up, so I went home and went to bed. I think I ate supper. I'm not quite sure.

When I wandered out of the bedroom, the Sunday and Monday *Star-Telegram*s were lying on the coffee table and Hal was rushing around trying to find his books in time to catch the school bus. Somnolently, I lifted the newspaper to find the books—I would like to be able to say that schoolbooks are not a standard feature of my coffee table, but actually they have been ever since Vickie started school—and then told him good-bye as he snatched the books and ran out the door. The bus driver was already honking. But he'd wait. He knows Hal.

Then I looked at the front page.

Harry did not bring me coffee. It seems I am off coffee for the duration, or else coffee is off me, however you want to put it. Who knows? I may never start drinking it again. That wouldn't be such a bad idea. It's gotten awfully expensive.

The usual custom, varied as necessary, is that Harry, who is at least halfway sane in the morning, makes breakfast; Hal sticks the dishes in the dishwasher after school; I make supper while Harry sleeps in front of the TV or runs around to get ready for a lodge meeting; and somebody—usually me—sticks the supper dishes in the dishwasher. The arrangement may or may not be fair to anyone. But it seems to work.

I looked at the paper and Harry brought me a raisin English muffin, toasted and dripping with butter, or rather with dietetic margarine, which is what I use right now. He also brought me a glass of milk.

I went on looking at the paper, wishing I could think of an acceptable (to myself, as well as to Captain Millner) excuse for staying home today. I did not want to go in. There would be reporters and I didn't have anything to say to them. They'd gotten hold of the story, all right. Boy, had they gotten hold of her story. The aging actress on the verge of a new television triumph (maybe somebody really had "suborned" the servants; there was no other place that could have come from)—life dogged by tragedy—the lovely young star expecting her first child, found unconscious in her wrecked car beside the lifeless body of her royal husband, whose hands were still locked on the wheel—many years later, expecting her second child, a glorious reconciliation destroyed when her husband's race car spun out of control, crashed, and burned before her horrified eyes—photos, old ones, nothing recent—Margali swathed in black at Forest Lawn; Margali, hands to face, at the racetrack; Margali dancing in a sequined evening gown—

Wait a minute. Wait a minute. What was it I had just read?

Ali Hassan was at the steering wheel when he died. Margali was beside him, on the passenger's side. And that wasn't some reporter's mistake, because here was an old news photo of Margali slumped against the glass while rescue workers with wrecking bars pried her out of the wreckage. It couldn't have been staged, not by Margali or anybody else, because the way that tree was wedged into the front of the car, whoever was driving had died instantly. I had seen the aftermath of enough accidents to know there was no possible doubt about that.

So Margali didn't kill Ali Hassan. So Jimmy was lying, or mistaken. And how do you get mistaken about something like that? Unless someone has misinformed you on purpose. But who? And why?

I sat across the desk from Captain Millner. "Damn," he said finally, "that's quite a little story."

"That's what I thought. And the fact that part of it isn't true doesn't make it all false."

"It wouldn't hurt just to check it out. Not that I know what the connection would be, but—"

But. This is called a fishing trip. Detectives go on a lot of fishing trips. You don't always—or even often, to tell the truth—know what you're going to reel in. Often you don't find anything at all. But every now and then you unexpectedly toss out a minnow and reel in a whale.

I needed to know as much as I could find out about Margali Bowman, not as I had seen her when I was a child, as a star miraculously landed on earth, too beautiful to be real, but as an all-too-mortal woman. I needed the ins and outs. And I didn't know whom to ask.

I couldn't ask her agent. Her agent was dead, or so I had been told.

I couldn't ask Sam because Sam was a suspect.

I didn't know who her best friends had been; I didn't know whether they were alive or dead.

Fara was a child when I was a child. Jimmy wasn't born yet.

In the end, I went over to the *Star-Telegram* office and asked for their file on Margali Bowman and, if they had one, on Sunny Messick.

Not surprisingly, both were checked out, to a feature writer named Everett MacCauley. The clerk told me where to find Everett MacCauley.

There must have been twenty desks in the long, rectangular, boxy room. They were all, without exception, messy—in-baskets and out-baskets all overflowing, desks piled with assortments of paper that surely nobody but the owner could make sense of. All very stereotypical, except that in place of typewriters, every desk now had a video-display terminal and a keyboard. Snakes of cable were everywhere, anchored with tape, disappearing behind trash cans, coiled under desks—just as we had been before the new police station was built, they were trying here to accommodate computer-age technology in a horse-and-buggy-age building.

Everett MacCauley, a professorial-looking man in his mid-forties, wearing corduroy slacks and a light blue shirt, welcomed me. Not, of course, to my surprise, he couldn't let me take the files with me, but he'd be glad to let me read through them there. "But the flow of information doesn't have to be one way, now does it?" he asked, with just a trace of put-on blarney.

"I can't tell you anything about the course of the investigation," I said. "And even if I could, we've barely had time to get started."

"But it was Miss Bowman's birthday," he said. "A birthday party. She was"—he consulted his notebook—"seventy-one."

"Really?" I'd actually thought she was a little older than that.

"Really. I," he said triumphantly, "have got her birth certificate." He thrust it at me.

She'd been born Marjorie Ruth Gorman, if this really was her birth certificate; and yes, he was right, she'd turned seventy-one last Friday. And this probably was her birth certificate—I remembered calling Fara's grandmother, Mrs. Gorman. She had been born at home; the birth had been normal; her parents— Frances Fay Lanham Gorman, housewife, and Andrew Mellon Gorman, bricklayer—had lived in Birdville, Tarrant County, Texas. That would be somewhere in the area that was now Richland Hills and North Richland Hills. She'd weighed seven pounds, three ounces, and she had been her mother's sixth child.

Born and died in Tarrant County, Texas. But she'd been a long way in the meantime. *You've come a long way, baby, to die where you were born.*

I handed the photocopy back, after noting the few vital statistics for which we might have a use. "Thank you," I said. "Now about the file—"

"What I want to know," MacCauley said, "is why you were at the party?"

"I'm an old friend of the family." That was the truth, of

course. Not the whole truth, but as much of the truth as I intended to give out.

We talked a little more, him fishing for information, me managing not to give much, and finally he gave up and handed me the two manila folders. Most of what was in them was supremely uninteresting—but not everything.

There was a clean cut in Sunny Messick's brake line on that day he had lost control on a curve in Indianapolis, Indiana. It might have been made by flying debris—the race car was virtually shattered—but then again it might have happened before the wreck. In which case, somebody had indisputably murdered Sunny Messick. But the problem was that nobody could say for sure. The investigation, as best as I could tell from the papers, had gradually petered out.

Well, I—like every other police officer—am more than a little acquainted with investigations that gradually peter out. Usually every possible lead has been chased into the ground and there's nowhere left to go, but every now and then there's that even more frustrating situation of "I know who did it, but I can't prove it."

Reading between the lines, there was a good chance that was what had happened in this case. The investigation had been complicated when Messick's chief mechanic, a fellow named Lew Mosier, died in what might have been an accident, a suicide, or murder.

Jimmy's account of Lew Mosier's death had been almost—but not quite—accurate.

Lew Mosier lived in a house trailer. He did his film developing—mostly pornographic shots of all his girlfriends, which in those days you couldn't get away with taking to your local drugstore for development—in his very small bathroom. Except for his enlarger, he kept his equipment and supplies in one cabinet in the kitchen. His few food staples—he mostly ate out—were in the adjoining cabinet.

The sugar was in an empty Peter Pan peanut butter jar with the label soaked off; it was identifiable by the lid.

So was the white crystalline cyanide.

A man not quite awake, maybe not quite sober, could—possibly—manage to confuse the two. It could have been an accident. But I didn't think it was.

Neither did the police then investigating Sunny Messick's death.

It could have been suicide. He could have felt to blame for Messick's death, whether or not he actually was, whether or not it was deliberate. But if it was suicide, he didn't leave a note.

It could have been murder. But if it was, not the least hint of a possible suspect ever had made it to the newspapers. Not that that was completely unusual; police prefer to keep such details to themselves, to prevent lawsuits, if for no other reason.

But to my mind—my trained cop's mind, which had suddenly cut on again, crowding home and husband and pregnancy out for the moment—the least little ghost of a pattern was beginning to emerge.

Question: What—really—had caused Ali Hassan's fatal accident?

Ali Hassan was a Moslem. Moslems aren't supposed to use alcohol. Most Moslems don't use alcohol.

This does not, of course, preclude the possibility that any one individual Moslem—particularly one habitually described in the staid prose of news stories as well as in the gossip columns as a "millionaire playboy"—may habitually use alcohol despite religious prohibitions. But most of the Moslems I've met take their religion pretty seriously.

Was Ali Hassan really drunk the night he crashed into the tree? Or was he drugged? And if so, with what? And by whom? The one person I knew it was not, despite Jimmy Messick's assertions, was Margali; because if Margali had doped her husband with the hope of causing a fatal collision, she certainly would not have then gotten in the car with him.

I asked MacCauley if he also had the file on Ali Hassan. He didn't, and wasn't sure there was one, except that of course Hassan had married Margali, and then, too, Hassan had died in Fort Worth. A fact I had not known until the file on Margali told me.

I thanked MacCauley, and returned to the morgue—newspaper morgue, not body morgue—to ask for the file on Ali Hassan.

There wasn't one.

But one thing there would have to be, if he'd died in Fort Worth, was a death certificate. I decided to go and get that, but first thought to call my office. That was fortunate, because Captain Millner was somewhat less than happy about my taking off without my radio. He informed me I had an appointment with Bob Campbell at one o'clock at Sam Lang's town house.

"What if I'm busy at one o'clock?" I asked.

"You will be," Millner told me. "With Bob Campbell."

Apparently I had no choice. But at least I did have time to go get the death certificate, though considering how recent, in real time, the death was, it seemed to me it took an indecent amount of time for anybody to locate and photocopy the document and turn it over to me.

But once I laid hands on it, it was very, very interesting. Ali Hassan had died with a bellyful not of alcohol, but of barbiturates mixed with orange juice.

I had a pattern.

I had a pattern, but Susan Braun still had the soldering iron, the hypodermic, the box of fire salts, and the cans of Diet Coke. I stopped by the closest pay phone and called Ident, to see which techs were in. Irene Loukas answered the phone. "Don't you ever sleep?" I asked her.

"Yeah, about as much as you do," Irene told me. "Whatcha need? Don't tell me you've got another corpse?"

"Not exactly," I answered. "Listen, do you know where the Braun Clinic is?" Irene allowed that she did, and I said, "Call over there and get Susan Braun on the phone. Tell her you need that sack of evidence we collected Saturday from Margali Bowman's bedroom, and—"

"Collected *Saturday*?" I could hear Irene's raised eyebrows. "She wasn't even dead Saturday."

"Collected Saturday," I repeated. "See whether she can take it to you or whether you should go get it. Don't let her send it by anybody else; I want to keep the chain of custody as tight as possible. When you get it, check for prints. You're looking for Margali's, Sam Lang's, or Robert Campbell's."

"I don't have prints from Lang or Campbell to compare," Irene objected.

"Then get them. Tell them you need to print them for elimination or something."

"And if they do, they do, and if they don't, they don't," Irene half-chanted in my ear.

"Right. If they do, they do, and if they don't, they don't. But try." Irene was right, of course. Nobody, unless he's actually been charged with a crime or is in one of the professions requiring fingerprinting and record checks, can be compelled to be fingerprinted.

What I was thinking was this: If Ali Hassan was murdered, drugs—an overdose so severe as to constitute poison—were involved in his death. If Sunny Messick was murdered, drugs may or may not have been involved; with a cut brake line and a corpse burned beyond recognition in full view of thousands of people, who's going to look for drugs? If Lew Mosier was murdered, he was certainly poisoned.

Margali had complained to me that she was being poisoned. And she was. Yes, we'd found the paraphernalia in her room.

But that didn't necessarily mean she was the one who'd put it there.

So—maybe someone tried poison first, only when it was difficult, such as maybe Sunny Messick might be hard to get at; or where it wasn't working, as with Margali Bowman, he'd move on to another method—one that would work, one that was sure.

Any one of five people could have killed Margali. But there was no way that Fara, or Edward Johnson, or Jimmy could have killed Ali Hassan, Sunny Messick, and/or Lew Mosier. That left Sam Lang or Robert Campbell. And for fairly obvious reasons, my money now was on Sam Lang.

Now the whole farrago of nonsense about wills—that multiplicity of wills, all supposed to be Margali's—made some sense, at least a small, frail amount of sense. If she had been afraid Sam would kill her; if she had been desperate to keep Sam guessing—

No, I didn't have any real, solid facts. What I had were a lot of good, strong hypotheses. And now was the time to go testing them.

I was walking as I thought; now I was back at the new police station, and I went up in the elevator—none of the elevators in the new police station have bullet holes in them, yet—in what Harry calls my "blue haze." I sat down at my desk and began to write notes to myself, explaining all these things to myself in case I forgot them.

Or, of course, in case somebody else had to pick up where I— inadvertently—left off. This sometimes happens in police work, and it's the pits to have to redo all of someone else's work. Particularly when you know you might not have the same background, or the same intuition, or even the same luck, as the person who did the work the first time.

Then I stopped and sat staring off into the stratosphere.

Nobody disturbed me, any more than I would disturb another

detective staring vacantly off into the stratosphere, until the phone rang. Dutch Van Flagg answered and then said, "Deb? For you."

It was Irene. "I thought you'd like to know," she said, "that there are no prints on any of this stuff."

"None? What about the cans?"

"None at all."

"Irene, three of us handled those cans. Susan and Fara and me. And none of us was wearing gloves or being especially careful. Our prints have got to be on them."

"Somebody wiped those cans thoroughly while they were still cold enough so that more water could condense on them after they were wiped. Then the water evaporated as the cans warmed up. The water spots took the fingerprint powder real good. There were a few places where I could make out the pattern of the towel, enough to tell it was velour with a jacquard pattern. New—not enough wear to be able to ident it. But no fingerprints, Deb. None at all."

"Thanks," I said, and dropped the phone back into the cradle.

That was impossible. Utterly impossible. Let's see, Fara got the Diet Cokes out. She took them to Susan and me and we both examined them. And then Sam came along and we had to think up something fast. So I went to lie down on Sam's bed. Susan had the cans then, but she brought them in a little later and set them down beside me.

Susan set them beside the bed and left and I went to sleep. I slept until Jimmy woke me. Somebody—anybody—could have gone in there without waking me, if he was quiet enough, cautious enough, knew the room well enough.

Knew Sam Lang's bedroom well enough.

And there was another opportunity. Jimmy and I were talking and Margali started screaming. I ran into her room. Jimmy was right behind me. I certainly didn't think of taking the cans with me then. I went back later to get them, of course, but how much later? Even I couldn't answer that. I had left them un-guarded in Sam Lang's bedroom.

Fingerprints are good, strong evidence. But so, sometimes, is the lack of fingerprints. It hadn't been Margali who'd rubbed those prints off.

I stood up. "Where are you going?" Millner asked me.

"To lunch. Then to meet with Bob Campbell."

There were racks of newspapers on the street. The story was first page on all of them, even *USA Today*. I'd figured Margali was old news. Nobody would remember her, except the people who knew her personally. But I was wrong. I had forgotten about VCRs; I had forgotten the renewed craze for old films.

It wasn't that raddled harridan clutching at me with dirty ring-bedecked paws, staggering drunk at the breakfast table, that the nation was mourning today. It was the glittering, curvaceous cutie who'd posed in a playsuit on the wing of a B-29.

And me?

Margaret, are you grieving/Over Goldengrove unleaving? . . . It is Margaret you mourn for.

Somebody made me read that once, when I was in school. Maybe I don't remember it right. Maybe that's not quite what it says.

I hated it when I had to read it. It didn't mean anything to me. And yet somehow it wouldn't go away, somehow it stuck in my mind and stayed and stayed and stayed, and now, today, I understood it. The tears I wiped away with the back of my hand, as I walked half-blindly into the coffee shop, weren't—really—for Margali.

They were for the little girl who had thought a movie star, a real, honest-to-goodness movie star, was the next best thing to a goddess on earth. Who had thought visiting a movie star's home was the most wonderful thing she could ever possibly do. Who childishly, blindly, openly, had adored Margali Bowman, not because she was so rich but because she was so beautiful and smelled so nice and had such a pretty voice.

The little girl had somehow, mysteriously, grown up to be me.

□ 9 □

WHY DO THINGS like this happen to me?

I had started out, three days ago, to go to a weekend party—a party where I was supposed to relax and have fun with old friends.

And now here I was trying to investigate four murders—if they were all murders—three of which had happened, if they had happened at all, either before I was born or while I was still young. On top of that, two of them were not only outside of my own jurisdiction of Fort Worth, but in fact totally out of the state of Texas.

Only one of them was my job. But I was afraid I had to clear the first three—at least in my own head—before I stood a chance of clearing the fourth.

Oh, shit. There were three television news trucks parked directly outside Sam Lang's driveway. That meant getting in would be like running the gauntlet, but at least I didn't have to do it on foot. Two uniformed patrol officers were standing guard at the end of the driveway.

No, they didn't recognize me. There are about 900 officers on the Fort Worth Police Department now, besides an assortment of civilian secretaries, clerks, and so forth. There was no reason that these two officers should recognize me. But they knew Sam Lang was expecting Detective Ralston, and when I identified myself, they waved me on through and then resumed their task of being something for news crews to photograph when there wasn't anything else going on.

Bob Campbell and Sam Lang were in the dining room, with a lot of paper spread out in front of them. Their almost identical expressions, as they looked up and saw me, suggested they'd have welcomed Dracula or Jack the Ripper, if he'd just tell them what to do with all these pieces of paper.

But I couldn't tell them that. The awful picture of the hunting dog and the pheasant was beating at my mind. Sunday it was the dog I noticed. Now it was the pheasant—the pheasant with the dead, blank eyes of Margali Bowman after her last friend failed her.

I looked away, sat down abruptly, and then saw the reason for the men's expressions. The papers on the table were Margali's wills.

Four of them.

Without preamble, Campbell asked me, "Did you and Margali talk about her will?"

"What makes you think we would have talked about her will?" I hedged.

"She trusted you," Sam said. "I don't think there were five people in the world Marjorie trusted. But you were one of them. If she talked to anybody, she talked to you."

My two suspects. But all the same Bob Campbell was her attorney and Sam Lang was her husband. Right now, until and unless I had made a real case against one or both of them, they had the right to know about her will.

"Yes, she did," I said.

"What did she tell you?"

"She was drunk. She was rambling quite a bit. But—" As well as I could, I gave the gist of what Margali had said.

When I had finished, Campbell asked, "Do you know which one of these she showed you?"

"None of them," I answered without hesitation.

"None of them?" Sam repeated incredulously.

But Bob—I might as well call him Bob now; I'd been calling him that all weekend—said, "That makes sense. Look, this is the first one I drew up for her, right after the marriage."

"That's the only one I ever knew about until today," Sam interjected. "Except those idiotic things she was always writing herself."

"But I drew up a second, last March. And it's not here."

"Okay, but what about those other three?" Sam demanded.

Bob shook his head. "I keep trying to tell you and you're just not understanding me."

"You're right. I'm not understanding you. So try again."

"These all are dated the same day, these three." He stacked the three newer-looking wills together. "They have different provisions. Unless we could find the attorneys who drew them up, and subpoena their appointment books, there's no way in hell we could tell which was signed last. But even if we could tell, we couldn't submit any of these for probate, because when she signed that one in March she revoked all previous wills, and—"

"But if we can't find the one she signed in March—don't you have a photocopy or something?"

"Oh, sure, I have a photocopy, but we can't submit it for probate because it's not a legal document. It's just a copy of—"

"But if you and the witnesses—whoever the witnesses are—"

"It won't work. We've got to find the one Margali actually signed. And that's where Deb's going to help us." He looked at me. "All right. You didn't have to pick up any of these to know it wasn't the one you saw. Why?"

"I told you. That one got wet."

"It could have had time to dry," Sam pointed out.

"Not damp. Wet," I repeated. "And look, you're assuming the one she showed me is the one you wrote for her in March. But that's not what she told me."

"You sure when she was talking about an attorney out of the phone book she wasn't meaning these earlier ones?"

"I'm sure."

"Then what did she tell you?"

I told him. Again.

"She found him in the phone book," Bob repeated. "Oh, hell." He rubbed his freckled forehead with a monogrammed handkerchief and thrust the handkerchief carelessly back into his pocket. "Do you know how many attorneys there are in the Fort Worth phone book?"

"Knowing Marjorie," Sam replied, "I figure his name's more likely to be Abbot than Zabrinskie."

"Unless she started in the middle. That's the trouble. That was always the trouble with Margali. You never knew what she was going to do."

"What difference does it make anyway?" I asked innocently. "I mean, Fara and Jimmy both told me she didn't have anything to leave."

Both men stared at me, with identical expressions of complete incredulity. It was Bob Campbell who found his voice first. "This is Texas!"

"What does that have to do with—"

"I can see you don't know much about Texas law."

"Only criminal law. That's all I'm supposed to know."

"Well, there's one more thing you better know, or your family's sure gonna be in a lot of trouble when you kick off." Sam, for a moment, sounded exactly like Jimmy, and I was somewhat startled.

Bob interrupted. "Let me explain. Do you know what 'community property law' means?"

I said I did, but my tone of voice and my face must have told a different story. "It means," Bob said, "that of all property acquired by a couple after their marriage, one half of it belongs to the wife and one half belongs to the husband."

"And Marjorie and I," Sam added, "were married about twelve years. This time." He sighed and repeated, "This time."

In the last twelve years, oil prices have gone crazy. Up and down, boom to bust and—in some places, but not Texas, this time—boom again. All this was about oil money, Sam's as well as Ali Hassan's. Twelve years ago was just after Harry finally got out of the service. I couldn't remember what prices were then; they'd started some kind of crazy upward spiral a few years earlier, so that groceries that had been costing me thirty-five dollars a week were suddenly costing sixty-five dollars, utilities that I'd budgeted as thirty-five dollars a month were suddenly spiraling toward one hundred dollars, and oil was leading the spiral.

At this moment we were sitting in a two-million-dollar mansion that wasn't ten years old. The Weatherford ranch—I knew Margali had bought it, with Sam's money, within the last five years. And all of a sudden Margali's will was very, very important, and all of a sudden a good two-thirds of my reasoning no longer made sense.

Because the fact that I didn't know something certainly couldn't be taken as proof that somebody else didn't know it—somebody else being Sam, who' apparently couldn't get rid of Margali by death or divorce without simultaneously losing half his fortune (unless her will was written to his specifications); or Jimmy, who'd probably never lay his hands on any money to speak of unless Margali died before Sam did; or Edward, who was clearly in Margali's good graces and might have decided the ends justified the means; or even Bob Campbell, who could (I didn't know, not without checking) be in real need of the massive legal fees he'd get for administering an estate this size.

I didn't really think that was likely, but I'd seen a TV show sort of like that just a few weeks ago.

So maybe the digging I was doing this morning didn't mean as much as I thought it meant. "Bob," I asked, as casually as I could, "do you know anything about Lew Mosier?"

He was fiddling with papers. He didn't stop; he didn't even pause. "Who's Lew Mosier? Am I supposed to?"

He'd answered my question. "What about you, Sam?"

There was a long silence. "Bob," Sam asked, "what's the statute of limitations on murder?"

"Well, in Texas—"

"No, I mean anywhere. Just anywhere at all."

Bob's puzzled expression was just barely short of comical. But he was a lawyer, and he'd been asked a legal question. "Well, there's not that much uniformity in criminal law from state to state. But, in general, there's no statute of limitations on murder. And even if there was—most people misunderstand the meaning of statute of limitations. Thing is—and again, this is in most states, not necessarily all—the statute of limitations doesn't go into effect until the perpetrator both has been identified and is located within the effective jurisdiction of the appropriate agencies."

"Put that in English."

"Well, say that in some state the statute of limitations on burglary is seven years. And John Doe breaks into Richard Roe's drugstore, and Richard Roe and two or three policemen saw him do it, and he left a real good fingerprint and it's identified right away, but for some reason or other—maybe some of the paperwork got misplaced or something like that—John Doe never got charged. Well, meanwhile he's turned his life right around, and ten years later he's running for mayor and his opponent digs back in the files and finds this old case and decides to take it to the Grand Jury. Well, he can't do that, because the statute of limitations has run out. But now say that fingerprint

is the only evidence and it isn't identified until ten years later—
or, say everybody knows John Doe did it but he's run off to
some country we don't have extradition treaties with and he's
just now come back—well, *now* he can still be prosecuted, even
if it is ten years later. Because if nobody knew who did it, or if
nobody could get at him to prosecute him, well, the statute of
limitations doesn't go into effect. Make sense?"

I could do without the constant "well." But Sam wasn't hearing that. He was just hearing the information, and now he nodded and said, "Yeah."

"Why'd you want to know?"

Sam didn't answer. He stared solemnly at me. "No, I don't
know anything about Lew Mosier." He kept staring at me.

"Why," I asked, "do you suppose a guy like Lew Mosier
would get killed?"

"Somebody must've not wanted him alive." He kept on staring at me and then, without warning, he burst into a broad grin
that once again was exactly like Jimmy's.

Right then I knew, as well as I know my own name, that Sam
Lang had paid Lew Mosier to kill Sunny Messick, and then he'd
personally murdered Lew Mosier, and I was pretty sure I knew
why. Sam Lang knew I knew it. And I'd never in a million years
be able to prove it, and Sam Lang knew I knew that too. And he
didn't care that I knew.

He ought to care. If he'd committed a more recent murder
that the old one was likely to lead me to, he ought to care that I
knew about the old one.

"What about Ali Hassan?" I asked.

"Ali Hassan? Damn fool was drunker'n a pissant and creamed
his car. Damn near took Marjorie with him—she was real
banged up. What do you want to know about him for?"

He didn't care that I knew he'd been responsible for two other
deaths. So—unless there was some very strong evidence that I

didn't know about—he wouldn't care if I knew about this one. If he'd done it.

I didn't think there was going to be any evidence, strong or otherwise. I was pretty sure Sam Lang was telling the truth. He thought Ali Hassan was drunk. He didn't know Ali Hassan was pumped full of barbiturates.

Which meant he didn't administer the barbiturates.

Which meant I didn't have a pattern at all. I just thought I did.

Which meant I was back to square one, with four (or five) possible suspects rather than one or two.

"Are we through with this discussion?" Bob asked loudly. "Because if we are, I want to get back to Margali's will. Deb, you're sure you'd recognize it?"

"No, I'm not sure. But I doubt there'll be more than one water-stained will with Margali's signature on it. And she had that one in her purse Saturday night at the bookstore."

"No she didn't," Sam said positively.

"I saw it there," I told him.

"You couldn't have because it wasn't there."

"But—"

"They let me look through her purse yesterday, with some policewoman watching me," Sam said. "There was a lot of stuff there, but there wasn't any will."

"So we need you to help us find it," Bob added, eyeing me hopefully. "So will you help us look for it?" Bob was the one who asked, but Sam's eyes were intent on me too.

I hesitated and then said, slowly, "Sam, I'm paid by the city of Fort Worth. And right now the city of Fort Worth is paying me to find out who killed Margali, not to help locate her will. But I can offer you a deal. If you'll sign a consent-to-search form, so that I can look for anything I might be able to use as evidence, I'll be glad to look for her will at the same time."

"You get your form and I'll sign it."

"I don't—really—think the will is in her bedroom," I said. "I'm telling you honestly, I am just about sure it is in her purse. But I'd like, for my own reasons, to start searching in her bedroom anyway." I was remembering that special hiding place she'd mentioned.

"Ma'am," Sam repeated, "I went down to your evidence vault and looked in her purse, and there wasn't no—any—will in it. You search wherever you want to search. You get that form and I'll sign it."

He was looking older, much older, than he had looked this weekend. He still had an LBJ air about him—not that he looked anything like LBJ; it was more in his massive size, in his air of unselfconscious arrogance—but now he was like LBJ after he had left the White House, a man who'd achieved the pinnacle and slid away from it and now was ready to die.

"Deb," he said now, "I know you're counting me as a suspect. You've got to. I know that. I know how many wives and husbands kill each other, and I know how me and Marjorie must've looked this weekend. But I want you to know something else. To start with, I'm older than Marjorie. I'm seventy-five."

He didn't look seventy-five. He looked, at an upward limit, about sixty. I told him so.

"I'm seventy-five," he repeated. "I've known Marjorie, literally, all her life. She was a sweet little thaing. Maybe if I'd put my foot down and kept her out of the pictures, she'd have been all right, maybe she wouldn't, it's hard to say now. But she was like a bird, a bright little bird flitting around here and there all nice and frisky, and you cain't clip a bird's wings. I tried to keep her safe but you cain't keep a bird safe without you keep it caged. So I let her fly and she scorched her wings and I tried to cage her and she broke her feathers beating against the cage."

"What's that supposed to mean?" I asked when Sam stopped for breath.

Sam grinned sheepishly. "I guess I mean she got her tail in a sling. That better? Everything she did she got her tail in a sling. I let her go; I let her have that divorce she wanted, or thought she wanted, and then she was in trouble all the time after that until I married her again. So I married her again and she walked out on me again and I got her back and tried to keep her safe and keep her from drinking and she turned into a lush because she was so bloomin' frustrated 'cause I just wouldn't let her get out and get into more trouble like she was in the habit of doing. Nothing I ever did was right. You want to know why I killed Sunny Messick?"

"You want to tell me?"

"I don't care if you know it. Nobody'd ever be able to prove it, and even if you could, what the hell, I'm seventy-five. It wasn't what you think. It wasn't because of Jimmy—just because of Jimmy. That was part of it, sure, but it wasn't all. Sunny taught her to drink. Before—the little ladylike sips of champagne, an occasional beer if the day was hot, that was all she wanted. Sunny taught her to drink whiskey. And Sunny taught her to drink hard; Sunny taught her to drink the way he drank. I'd seen her with Sunny falling down drunk. I thought—I thought if I got Sunny away from her she'd quit drinking."

"And that's the only reason?"

"Hell, no, that's not the only reason. But it's reason enough. I thought she'd quit drinking. I was wrong, of course."

I didn't say anything. Neither did Bob, and after a moment Sam started talking again.

"She didn't quit. She just got crazier and crazier and crazier—and—and I'm lying to you."

"You're lying to me? Lying how?"

"Yeah. I'm lying to you. I didn't kill Sunny Messick." And in front of me, in front of Bob Campbell, the big tough would-be LBJ clone started to cry. "I guess I better tell you the truth. It might—I don't know how. But it might matter now. I don't know how it would, but it might. I told myself for so many years that if anybody ever found out, I'd take the blame. But it doesn't really matter now. I didn't kill him, but I would have. I was ready to kill him, I just didn't get the chance. Lew Mosier, the mechanic, did. Of course. Marjorie—I don't know how Marjorie talked him into it but somehow she did. And she came to me later. He was bleeding her white."

"Blackmail?" Bob asked. I shushed him with a gesture.

"Blackmail. He'd taken everything she had, everything, and he was trying to get his hands on Fara's money, and Marjorie'd have given it to him, too, only she couldn't figure out how to get it out of the trustees' hands. So—I went over and I had me a little talk with Lew Mosier. I didn't know what I was going to do. I mean I knew what I was going to do but I didn't know how yet. I thought I might just shoot him or something. He gave me a better idea. Thing is, he was drunk. He had his darkroom gear all out on the table. He was just putting it away. We were—we were talking. Just talking. Good-ole-boy talk. I could always get people to talk to me, men, I mean, that is. Well, mostly women too, but especially men because I look like just another good ole boy. And Lew, he didn't know who I was. And he kept showing me the pictures he'd been printing. Pictures—of Marjorie. He thought it was real funny. And I let him laugh—then—because I didn't have my gun along and I didn't want to fight him, a little shrimpy guy like that; I'm twice his size. So I helped him put his stuff away, and then I asked him what you use sugar for in the darkroom, when I saw that jar, and he laughed and told me it wasn't sugar. He told me what it was. He told me he better not ever get the two mixed up. And he kept on drinking. It was about five A.M. by then and he was still drinking and laughing and talking about women, including Marjorie. And then he went to the bathroom. He went to the bathroom and I switched the jars. That's all. And then he came back and started making coffee and I told him I had to leave."

And that was why the bed was made. That simple. He'd never gotten in it that night.

"Why did you think it was sugar? When you asked him, I mean?"

"It looked to me like sugar. And you know, lots of people keep sugar in peanut butter jars."

That was perfectly true; I'd done it myself until we finally got air conditioning. But—"Why in the world would he have had the jar of developing chemicals and the jar of sugar that close to each other, then, if they looked that much alike? That doesn't make sense. He could have had an accident with them even without—uh—help."

"You know how to develop pictures?"

"No, why?"

"It takes a lot of stuff—a lot of chemicals, and a lot of supplies, and a lot of equipment. You ever try to do anything in a trailer?"

"I've lived in a trailer." I was beginning to see what he was leading up to, but it still didn't make much sense.

"He developed in the bathroom because that was the only place dark enough. But he stored everything in this one cabinet in the kitchen because it was the only place he had to store it in. So I watched him put everything away—even helped him, a little—and then he shut that door marked STAY OUT—CHEMICALS! and then he went to the bathroom and there was that sugar jar on the table about four feet away and that cyanide stuff in the closed cabinet and I just—switched 'em. That's all. He wouldn't have had an accident without I helped. And he'd have gone right on bleeding Marjorie to death."

"You wouldn't fight him because he was half your size but you left him to die of cyanide poisoning."

"Put that way it does sound kind of odd, doesn't it? But I guess I was drunk too." Sam rubbed his eyes. "I guess I was drunk too. But—the question you didn't ask. No. I didn't kill

Marjorie. I wouldn't hurt Marjorie. I haven't been liking her much these last few years. I haven't been liking her much, not the way she'd gotten to be, but I always did love her."

"Sam, you know I've got to let the Indiana police know about this."

"Go ahead. You just go right ahead, little lady. But you never warned me of my rights." From tears, he went abruptly to laughter. "I watch television too, sometimes. I know how things are supposed to work. And you never did warn me of my rights."

He was right. I hadn't thought to warn him of his rights. Neither had Bob Campbell, who was sitting right beside him listening to him confess to murder.

"Sam," I said, "I want to change the subject a little. The night Ali Hassan wrecked his car—you said he was drunk. Were you going by newspaper accounts, or by what Margali said, or did you see him yourself?"

"I saw him. It was a party, and—all right, I didn't know Ali Hassan except by sight. I didn't want to know him. But it was one of those let's-all-be-all-civilized invitations, you know, friends of Marjorie and friends of mine both, so they'd invited us both to show they weren't taking sides. Which was kind of dumb, if you ask me, but I had to be all noble, so I went. And— I don't know what Hassan was drinking. He started out with orange juice and then switched to something else. Whiskey and soda, I guess. It looked like whiskey and soda."

"Or like ginger ale?" I asked. Moslems—in general—don't drink. And the autopsy hadn't found any alcohol in him.

"Well, you know, a weak whiskey and soda, it looks like ginger ale. Anyhow, he and Marjorie were getting along together real good. Too damn good for my tastes. And then Hassan said he didn't feel so good and he wanted to go home, and Marjorie said she didn't want to go yet, he could go by himself and she'd get a ride, and he told her she'd be a decent wife and go with him. By that time they was yelling at each other by the front door. I turned around for a minute—somebody was trying to talk to me and I was trying to tell him to shut up—and then Marjorie screamed and I looked around and damned if he wasn't dragging her out the door. Had grabbed her by the wrist and she was kicking and scratching at him with the other hand and he wasn't paying her no mind, just went right on dragging her. Everybody tried to rush that way, and time I could get to the door they was out of sight. I went after them—I didn't care if he was her husband, he didn't have no call to manhandle her like that—and he crashed the car before he got good and out of the driveway. It was a long driveway and he was driving like a bat out of hell—accelerating all the way—and he couldn't make the turn around that big ol' tree. I mean I saw him crash the car. And I got there and Hassan was plumb dead with the steering column through his chest the way butterfly collectors put pins in butterflies, and Marjorie was out cold. I tried to get her out of the car but I couldn't and then somebody must've called the police because they got there and—"

"That's all I need," I interrupted. "Thank you. You've been very informative."

He grinned Jimmy's lopsided grin at me. "You still going to tell Indiana?"

"Probably. Oh, I don't know. Maybe I won't. After all, I didn't read you your rights." Rights or no rights, who's going to prosecute a seventy-five-year-old man for killing a blackmailer twenty-seven years ago? Sure, I'd tell Indiana, just so they could mark it cleared. But nobody was going to do anything about it. "Speaking of rights—"

I got a consent-to-search form out of the briefcase I have to haul around when I'm officially working a case. He signed it, Bob witnessed it, and then, as I was returning it to the briefcase, I asked as casually as if it were an afterthought, "Sam, what do you usually drink?"

"Bourbon, mostly."

"I mean is there anything you drink that comes in cans?"

He stared at me and shook his head.

"No Cokes? Ginger ale? Beer? Nothing like that?"

He shook his head again. "Why?"

I didn't start searching in Margali's room after all. I started searching in Sam's room. Yes, Margali had babbled to me about a hiding place for her will. But where would it be? Keeping Sam alive took priority now. Because if he wasn't the killer, then there was a good chance someone was trying to kill him. There was an open bottle of bourbon on top of the bar in his bedroom. I took it. Very carefully, so as to be able to check for fingerprints.

In his clothes closet, on the floor under his shirts, was a cardboard case containing five more bottles of bourbon. Four of them were sealed. Completely sealed. I studied them carefully and couldn't find any way they could have been opened.

The fifth wasn't quite sealed. It had been opened. Extremely carefully, so that the paper seal on the neck hadn't torn. But the attempt to reglue the lower part of the paper seal hadn't quite worked.

There was sediment visible at the bottom.

Margali had killed two of her husbands. At least two. Did "that singer" Jimmy told me about really kill himself? Did Margali throw the bottle of Aramis through the plate glass window because she wanted to kill Cal—whoever Cal was—and couldn't get her hands on him because she'd already thrown him out?

Margali was trying to kill Sam because Sam was trying to keep her safe. Keep her safe. Keep her caged. She'd set the stage so very carefully. The Diet Cokes. The tampered-with Diet Cokes. "Somebody's trying to poison me." Sooner or later, if she had kept raising enough fuss, somebody would have found the Diet Cokes. Poor Margali. Somebody is trying to kill Margali. Take her away where she'll be safe.

Meanwhile Sam would have gone on drinking his bourbon, quite routinely, a shot or two a night, and one night he'd have gotten down to the bottom of the bottle with the sediment in it, or maybe he'd have sloshed it around and stirred up the sediment.

Either way, poor Sam. Whoever had tried to get Margali would have gotten Sam.

And Margali wouldn't even have been there.

My dear old friend Margali was as heartless a murderer as I'd ever come across in my life . . . if I was right. But I wasn't quite sure yet that I was.

But all the same, my dear old friend Margali was dead. And I wasn't one inch closer to finding out who had killed her.

Margali's room. Not that I expected to find anything useful.

Jimmy's room. Because how had Jimmy known those long-kept secrets he had told me—had told me in a scrambled form, had told me almost but not quite right, but had told me? Had told me enough to put me on the right track.

Or maybe not quite the right track.

Considering I'd just helped to clean Margali's room two days before, I doubted there would be much in it I hadn't already seen. But on the other hand, there was that big walk-in closet I'd hardly touched; the safe I'd seen only the surface of; that huge bathroom with one wall completely composed of drawers and doors.

What was I looking for? I'd better make a list, before I even called myself through with Sam's room.

I was looking for: anything that could make an ice-pick-shaped hole in the back of someone's brain; anything that could explain why Margali thought she had a starring role in an up-coming television series—because I was sure she really believed that; it wasn't part of her playacting; anything that could explain why Jimmy got even a distortedly accurate idea of how Hassan and Messick died.

Sanchita? The housekeeper? I'd better talk with Sanchita. Fara said she'd been here forever. Did she mean here in this house, in which case forever was less than ten years, or did she mean here with either Margali or Sam, in which case forever could mean—well, a very long time.

I couldn't remember knowing Sanchita when I was a girl visiting Margali. But that didn't mean Sanchita wasn't there. There were housekeepers; there were always housekeepers. I just never heard their names, at least not to remember.

What else was I looking for? I didn't really know. Anything that I could find that would help me make sense out of this increasingly bizarre situation.

The first thing I found didn't take me long. They were in a drawer in the bathroom. A stack of letters ostensibly from a Hollywood agent. And it was surprising that even Margali could have been fooled for long.

I sat down on the floor and read the first few. The second was an elaborate apology. "I am in the process of moving my office and the telephones are unhooked both places. I'll give you a telephone number as soon as one is available. Again, let me apologize for your distress when you were unable to get the number from information."

He didn't have a telephone but he was able to get her an offer from a major producer? Come on.

And the confusion of the letters—the lack of coherent sequencing—gave me a hunch where they had come from.

They hadn't come from somebody who was used to business letters. Sam was used to business letters.

They hadn't come from somebody who was used to putting together coherent thought. And an evangelist—no matter how odd his church seemed to me—had to be able to put together sermons and appeals for donations. These letters hadn't come from Fara or Edward Johnson.

They certainly hadn't come from somebody with the presumably disciplined mind of an attorney.

But they had come from somebody with at least a little knowledge of acting, of talent agencies, of the way shows are put together.

That meant there was only one person on my suspect list that could have written those letters. And that person was Jimmy Messick.

But the fact that he had been conning his mother didn't mean he had killed his mother. I went on looking.

I didn't find anything that could have any connection with the crime, not anything at all, and it got to be four o'clock, and it got to be five o'clock, and it got to be six o'clock, and Captain Millner called me at Sam Lang's house.

"Deb, I suggest you go home."

"I'm not through yet." The department has calmed down from the early effects of the Supreme Court decision on police overtime, and superior officers no longer run feverishly around the building at shift change ordering people to leave at once.

"Deb, I suggest you go home."

"But—"

"Deb, if you are in the condition that I strongly suspect that your are in, you need more rest than you're getting. I don't want you off duty any longer than you have to be."

"What?"

"You heard me. Deb, go home."

"All right," I said meekly.

"Oh, by the way," and there was a slightly malicious tone in his voice, "your son called. I am to instruct you that Harry went to the lodge and you're out of toilet paper."

"What?"

"You heard me."

"Hasn't he ever heard of Stop and Go? He wastes half his allowance there playing video games. He could get on his bicycle and go get some toilet paper himself."

"I suggested that. He said he'd spent his allowance already."

"What on?" I asked mechanically. "He just got it."

"I didn't ask that, though your video-game suggestion sounds likely. They tell me K-Mart has a good selection of toilet paper."

I hung up.

But I didn't go to K-Mart. If Hal was that desperate, he could use Kleenex.

Because I was thinking, I couldn't stop thinking, and I couldn't make my thoughts make sense.

It was Sam who'd killed Margali.

Or it was Jimmy who'd killed Margali.

Or it was Fara—my old friend Fara—who'd killed Margali.

Or it was Fara's husband, evangelist Edward Johnson, who'd killed Margali.

All four were possible. All four were—let's face it—even likely.

Just because Sam had semiconfessed to one murder, and confessed and then withdrawn the confession to another, didn't mean he hadn't committed another, more recent, murder. Or, for that matter, another one before those.

If the same person killed Margali's second and third husbands, and a mechanic who'd worked on a race car (and been the weapon—sort of—for one of those murders), and also Margali, then that person wasn't Fara or Jimmy or Edward. But I couldn't assume the same killer.

Another thing I couldn't assume was that just because I didn't understand how important Margali's will was, other people also didn't understand—no matter who the other people were, no matter what the other people had told me.

Jimmy. He might—or might not—be Sam Lang's son. He

might—or might not—figure in Sam Lang's will. He might—or might not—be in Margali's will. And he might—or might not—want Margali's (and, for that matter, Sam's) money enough to kill for it.

He didn't have a weapon that night at the Blue Owl. He had a ballpoint pen and a key ring. You couldn't kill anybody with either of those. Well, actually, you probably could, but the resultant damage would bear not the remotest resemblance to a hole made by an ice pick.

Fara. She had enough money now. But her children, if she should die, would be left dependent on the collection plate of the Evangelical Church of the—whatever. Fara's trust would revert back to her father's relatives on her death. She'd told me that.

She didn't have a weapon either. She had a rat-tail comb. You could, I suppose, if you were desperate enough, stab somebody to death with a rat-tail comb. But not easily. Not without the person having time to make a lot of noise.

Edward. He had Fara's money—now. But if his bossiness ever got to her—if she ever left him—what then?

Was he in Margali's will?

Or even if he felt secure enough never even to consider the possibility of Fara leaving him, were the little girls in Margali's will?

Was his church in Margali's will?

For Edward, would the end justify the means?

I went to Fara's house.

Edward ordered me out exactly eight minutes later. By then Fara was in tears again; the two little girls, who'd been sent to their rooms on my arrival, were back, flanking their mother and staring wide-eyed at me; and Edward, in a towering rage, was quoting Scripture at me. I think it was Jeremiah.

So I left and went to K-Mart. It is, after all, on the way home.

I bought a new pillow, that awful cat—I swear I'm going to get Olead to take that cat—having been highly indiscreet on Hal's pillow.

I bought some squirt soap. Harry is always running out of squirt soap. Sometimes I think he eats it.

I bought some nail polish remover and nail polish. Maybe bright red nail polish will distract people's attention from my midsection.

And I said the hell with it and bought four pair of maternity slacks and four tops and two A-line dresses.

And, of course, the toilet paper.

At the checkout stand, the cashier and I engaged in a highly acrimonious discussion as to which pillow was on special. It turned out, after a five-minute debate during which we both went to look at the pillows, that he was right that the one I had in my cart wasn't on sale. But on the other hand, my extreme confusion was quite understandable, in view of the fact that the SALE sign had been placed neatly and prominently over the wrong stack of pillows.

We talked some more as he checked everything out and tossed the rejected pillow over into a large stack of other rejected merchandise from, I suppose, the whole day. I assured him that I knew it wasn't his fault and I wasn't mad at him, but I was very annoyed at the moron who'd put the sign in the wrong place.

He tossed something else over into the rejected pile. I didn't notice what it was as it went by, and I don't think he quite noticed that he was putting it there instead of in my shopping cart.

I got home with a different new pillow, some squirt soap, nail polish and polish remover, four maternity slacks and four maternity tops, two A-line dresses, and no toilet paper. That was when I realized what the other thing that had been tossed over into the rejected pile—after its price was read onto my bill by the little scanner—was.

I called the manager of K-Mart. I was neither friendly nor polite. And then I went back out to Stop and Go and bought some toilet paper.

Why do things like this always happen to me when I don't have the time or the energy to cope with them?

· 10 ·

I CALMED DOWN LATER, of course, and felt like a real idiot for making such a fuss over a four-pack of toilet paper. But of course it wasn't the toilet paper I was really upset about; it was the combined weight of everything that had happened since Friday night, and the unfortunate assistant manager at K-Mart just happened to catch me when I was ready to blow up anyway.

Monday night is bingo night at the lodge, but Harry wasn't scheduled to call and he hates to play it, so I thought maybe he was just at some kind of committee meeting and he'd get home after a while. I guessed I had better make supper. But what? Kind of a chilly night—a chili night? Homemade chili with cornbread? That's fast.

And Hal wouldn't disturb me. He was in his bedroom doing homework. He is, by fits and starts, becoming a little more responsible about his homework.

I guessed right. Harry wandered in before I got the cornbread into the oven. When I closed the oven door and returned to the living room, he was sitting on the floor in front of his radio table sorting magazines and catalogs. He does this about once in six months. For some reason we can't quite fathom, except that it might have something to do with his subscription to *Soldier of*

Fortune, he has gotten on the mailing list of dozens of survivalist firms, arms dealers, and you name it.

When we are to the point of being ankle-deep in catalogs, he cleans them all out and generously gives them to me to read.

Usually I don't. Usually I wait until he's not looking, bundle them all up, and haul them off along with the dead newspapers to whoever's collecting scrap paper for charity that particular week. But today I decided what the heck, I was in a crummy mood anyway, I might as well leaf through a catalog or two.

Look, whatever Harry thinks, I did not deliberately let the cornbread burn. I'm not that eager to go out to eat. After all, I'm the one who has to scrub the pan, and if you haven't tried to scrub burnt cornbread out of a cast-iron pan lately—well.

It was just that advertisement. I won't tell you what catalog it was in. I won't tell you the name of the product. I don't want you to go out and buy one. It ought to be illegal. It's a murder weapon pure and simple and not another thing but; it has no earthly use for either defense or sport.

It looks like a nice, neat, harmless ballpoint pen. It carries easily in a pocket or purse—just like that nice, neat ballpoint pen Jimmy Messick had in his pocket that night at the Blue Owl—that nice, neat ballpoint pen he was carrying with no notebook, no scratch pad, no checkbook, nothing at all to write on. But let me give you the rest of the description. "Instant defense with the press of a clip. Ordnance steel construction. Spring-loaded 4″ shaft instantly locks into full extension when you need it." It was normally priced at $28.95 but the sale price was only $22.95. Goodie, goodie, I thought, cut-rate homicide.

Because that was all it was, homicide for sale. There was no possible way it could be used for defense, no matter what the ad said.

So now I knew who. At least I thought I knew who.

It all fitted together very nicely. There were the letters—Jimmy was the only one in the household who'd actually come in contact with any kind of talent agency. There was a motive of sorts, if he thought (rightly or wrongly) either that he was Sam's son or that Sam thought he was, and if he thought Margali was going to tell Sam he wasn't.

And now, there was a weapon.

Maybe.

Maybe.

But I knew that despite his rather wimpy appearance he was an outdoorsman of sorts. He and Olead used to go camping together. As an outdoorsman, he'd very likely get the same type of junk mail Harry got. And a weapon of this sort would appeal to the kind of devious mind that would convince a hopeless alcoholic that she had a television role forthcoming—would think it was funny to put Ex-Lax out as Christmas candy—would put Epsom salts in the stew.

Yes, I was reaching. It's a far cry from fraud to murder. But then, it's a far cry from practical joking to fraud. And that was a line I just about knew he'd crossed.

Maybe I was wrong. But then again, maybe I wasn't. The next step was to think of a way to persuade Jimmy to show me that alleged ballpoint pen he had. And that, if I was right, wasn't going to be easy.

It was at this point in my musings, as I was wondering how, in the event that I was right, I would ever be able to prove it, that Hal wandered in and watched me alternately staring at the catalog and gazing off into space, waited a moment, and then said, "Mom, something in the kitchen sure does smell funny."

"Oh, no!" I yelped, and catapulted off the couch and dashed into the kitchen. Somewhat too late. The cornbread was somewhat darker brown than it was supposed to be and the chili was sort of glued to the bottom of the pan.

So I went and put on one of my new outfits and Harry resignedly took Hal and me out to the Red Lobster for dinner.

I don't remember what I ate.

When I got home I called Susan. There were two things I wanted to ask her. She was sure about the first. "If you'd asked me to start with," she said, "I could have saved you a lot of trouble. Margali came to me—patient to doctor—off and on for about six months, and—"

"Why didn't you tell me sooner?" I interrupted. "Like while she was still alive?"

"I couldn't, Deb, you know that." Of course I did know that. Susan and I were friends, but that friendship couldn't allow either of us to forget professional obligations.

"Okay, so what did she tell you about wills?"

"Can we just say I've got a drawer full of Margali's wills? She made them constantly, Deb. Most of them were holograph and didn't begin to conform to legal requirements, and they're not worth anything. Every now and then she'd find an attorney to draw one up. I don't think she knew—or understood—about community property laws, though. It's just that in her mind she was still a big star. In her mind her old movies—which she didn't even own residual rights on—were still important, valuable. And she rewrote her will constantly."

"Did—does—Sam know that? Or Jimmy?" I knew Fara did. She'd mentioned it, and I hadn't paid it the attention it deserved.

"I don't know. I should think they probably did."

"About the other—"

"I can't, Deb. I can't tell you that."

"Why can't you?"

"Because Jimmy's still alive. He's still my patient. Look, why don't you ask Olead? He used to know Jimmy better than just about anybody else."

I called Olead. He was hesitant; he didn't want to say Jimmy could be a killer. He and Jimmy had been through too much together. On top of that, not a year ago Olead's mother had been murdered; now it was Jimmy's mother, and Olead was sorry for him. But I kept prodding, and finally, reluctantly, he said, "Look, Jimmy used to talk about ways of killing people. He used to say stab 'em in the brain, it's fast, it's quiet. But Deb, that doesn't mean he'd really do it."

"But do you think he would?"

A long silence. "Deb, I don't know. I just don't know . . . yeah, I guess he would. If he wanted to. If he really wanted to."

"How strong a reason would he need?"

Another long silence. "He wouldn't need a reason. Jimmy doesn't ever need reasons. He—he just would need to think it might be fun."

I went to bed. I didn't sleep very well. Somebody who might murder his mother because it might be fun. . . .

Defiantly, I wore one of my new outfits to the office Tuesday. Nobody commented on it at all. They didn't even tease me. The most reaction I got was from Dutch Van Flagg, and all he said was, "That's what I thought."

I'd have gotten mad if they had teased me. So why was I feeling disappointed—even, in a way, insulted—that they didn't? Oh, well, I can't be logical all the time. I have enough trouble being logical about work, where it counts.

Captain Millner didn't seem too sure I was being logical even about my work. "That's mighty flimsy reasoning," he told me. "You saw a gadget in a catalog. Messick had a pen in his pocket and nothing to write on. That proves Messick's pen was your gadget and Messick killed his mother?"

"It's not just that," I argued. "It's the letters too."

"It's still mighty flimsy reasoning."

Of course it was flimsy reasoning. I hadn't proven anything, even to myself. But it was a hunch, a hypothesis. And I at least thought it was a darn good hunch.

A good-enough hunch that when I drove through Sam Lang's gateway half an hour later, I stopped and asked one of the patrolmen—the bigger one—to go with me.

We were down to two TV trucks now, and only a small scattering of other reporters. But all that were left eagerly took pictures of the burly patrolman getting into my detective car. What they intended to do with the pictures escapes me utterly, and will continue forever to do so, because I didn't watch the news that night.

Inside, I found Sam Lang and Bob Campbell methodically taking apart the den, or projection room, or whatever you want to call it. I suppose they didn't dare trust most of the servants to understand what it was they were looking for. They did have Sanchita with them. I recognized her. I didn't remember her until this moment; I didn't know I knew her, but I recognized her. Stolid, emotionless, ageless. She'd been there, exactly the same age she was now, a silent figure in the background washing things and putting them away, when I was twelve years old. How could I have forgotten her?

"Hello, Sanchita," I said.

She nodded to me gravely.

I waited a few minutes, the patrolman fidgeting a little behind me, and then asked, "Sam, is Jimmy around?"

"In his room, why?"

"Well—" Oh, no, was I picking up the "well" habit from Bob Campbell? I'd just managed to get rid of "y'know." "Since he's an adult, I need to get a separate consent-to-search from him before I can get into his room. Your consent isn't enough, even though you own the house, since that space is provided to him for his personal use. Do you think he'll object?"

"Why in the world would he want to object?"

"Then I need you or Bob, one or the other, to witness his signature."

Bob straightened, looking at the patrolman. "Can't he do it?" he demanded, holding his right hand to what was apparently an aching back.

"Well, he could, but it would be better if it was you or Sam."

In the end, they both decided to come. That was what I really wanted anyhow.

Jimmy Messick was lying on his back on a neatly made double bed, hands under his head and a stereo turned up loud. He was staring vacantly at the ceiling. He turned his head when the door opened, and although he immediately got up and turned the stereo off, I'd seen the slight flicker of unease, of fear, when I entered with a uniformed patrolman right behind me. Of course anybody could be alarmed, even frightened, when two police officers enter his bedroom at nine o'clock in the morning. But all the same, I didn't think I was wrong.

The pen—alleged—was in the front pocket of his shirt.

I got the consent-to-search form out of my briefcase and explained what it was and why I needed his signature.

Jimmy stared at the form. "What'll happen if I don't sign it?"

"Then, of course, I'll go get a search warrant." That was bluff. I didn't have probable cause and I knew it. Probably so did Bob Campbell, even though he wasn't a criminal lawyer. But he didn't tell Jimmy.

Jimmy continued to stare at me. His eyes shifted to Sam, to Bob, and then back to me. "Can I go to the bathroom?" he asked.

There wasn't a bathroom attached to his room; I knew that because there were only two doors out of his room and they were both open. One led to the hall, the other to a crowded and messy closet. "Sure, go to the bathroom all you want," I said. "I'll even station a patrolman in the hall—since Sam's given me consent to search the rest of the house—to see you get there safely."

He sat quite still for a moment. Then he said, "I guess I might as well sign it, then."

"I guess you might as well," I agreed sweetly. I deliberately did not get out a pen. Instead, I asked to borrow Jimmy's.

There was another long silence. By the time he said, "It's not writing right now," both Sam and Bob were offering me pens.

I took Bob's and filled out the form. Jimmy signed it. Bob witnessed it and put his pen back into his pocket.

Then I asked, "If your pen doesn't write, why are you carrying it around with you?"

The answer came faster this time. "I keep meaning to take it by an office-supply shop and get it a refill, but I keep forgetting to do it, so I thought maybe if I stuck it in my pocket—"

"May I see it?" I asked. "Maybe I can get it to work."

He knew, then. He might have known already, or at least guessed, but now he knew. He looked at Sam. He looked at the uniformed officer, who was shifting position behind me. And then he took the pen out of his pocket and very quietly handed it to me.

He wasn't twitching now. He sat still on the bed, perfectly still, and watched me. By now the room had gone completely silent. They all knew there was something wrong—something seriously wrong—but only Jimmy and I knew what, until I found the right button and pushed it and the gleaming four-inch blade shot out.

No, blade isn't the right word. Blade implies a cutting edge, and this wasn't a cutting edge. It had a sharp, sharp point, and the rest of it was smooth. Jet smooth. Streamline smooth.

And gleaming isn't quite right either, because the gleam was spoiled, here and there, by smudges of brownish-red tarnish.

He didn't—quite—get it clean.

I don't know how much longer the body that calls itself Sam Lang will go on walking around. He might see seventy-six, though I doubt it. He won't make seventy-seven. Because right then, at that moment, I saw the essence that made that body Sam Lang shrivel up and die.

I was the one who asked the question Sam Lang didn't, after I gave the perfectly inevitable warning. "You want to tell me why?"

Jimmy Messick grinned at me, but the grin didn't seem quite real. "Find out," he said.

"I mean, with that extra will floating around, it seems to me you'd have been safer with her alive." That was a blow at a venture; I was hoping he would tell me what—worth killing for—the will contained.

He didn't.

"It wasn't true. But she'd have said it was—" He'd said too much. He stopped, licked his lips, looked at Sam. "It wasn't true. But she threw a lot of wills away. I thought she threw that one away too. I thought she was going to make another one like it. She didn't. Did she?"

"If she did, we haven't found it."

Sam found his voice. "What are you talking about?"

Jimmy didn't answer. I did, but not the way he wanted me to. I just said, "It doesn't matter now. It doesn't matter now, Sam, at all." I hoped it didn't. We'd probably find out eventually.

I don't know when Sanchita entered the room. But there she was standing in the doorway behind me, and although I can't recall ever hearing her voice before, I recognized it as soon as she spoke. Without as much of an accent as I would have expected, she said, "The fathers have eaten sour grapes and the children's teeth are set on edge."

Without turning, I asked, "Sanchita, was it you who told Jimmy about his and Fara's fathers?"

Almost scornfully, she answered, "Sunny Messick was not Jimmy's father. But yes, I told him. He had the right to know. I told Fara too. She said I was lying. But Edward—Reverend Johnson—he believed me. I am saved by the blood of the Risen Redeemer."

"Does that mean you go to Edward's church?"

"I live in the arms of the Risen Redeemer and Edward Johnson speaks for the Risen Redeemer whose very name is truth."

"That doesn't mean Edward Johnson's name is truth. Or yours. Not everything you told Jimmy was correct."

"Enough of it was."

"You told Jimmy his mother killed Lew Mosier."

"Who do you think killed Lew Mosier?"

"I know who killed Lew Mosier. It wasn't Margali."

Jimmy's eyes kept going back and forth between me and Sanchita. I kept watching him; I never turned to look at Sanchita, so I don't know what the expression was on her face when she said, "It was not Margali's hands, but it was Margali's evil heart. She hated men. She hated all men. That's why she hated her son. He was going to grow up to be a man. She took care of that. That one, he will never be a man."

"That's not true!" Jimmy shouted, and dived off the bed toward Sanchita, his hands outstretched. He dodged past me, and the patrolman—his name tag said his name was Kent—grabbed him. Jimmy stopped then and stood panting, and Kent turned him around to handcuff and frisk him.

"That's not true," Jimmy said again, more quietly.

"Enough of it was true," Sanchita said.

Enough of it. That was true. "Book him in at the city jail on a charge of capital murder," I told Kent. "I'll go in later to swear out a warrant."

Kent finished patting him down. There weren't any other weapons on him. The pen was the only one he had.

"Hey, Campbell," Jimmy said, "call my psychiatrist, would you? Her name is Susan Braun." And this time Jimmy's slow grin was natural and real. "You really think you're going to get a conviction?" he asked me.

I could have laughed. I could have cried.

I did neither. I searched Jimmy Messick's bedroom, thoroughly.

I found a stack of *Soldier of Fortune* magazines, hunting magazines, camping-gear and survivalist-gear catalogs. Nothing illegal, improper, or, in the Southwest, unexpected about any of that; nothing in it I couldn't find any day of the week under my own husband's radio table.

I found a stack of printed stationery that matched the letterhead from Margali's new agent, who'd promised her the wonderful new TV show, and with it was a bill from a remailing service in Beverly Hills. But in all the letters from him Margali had kept, he'd never once asked for money, so I couldn't even charge him with fraud on those. He'd have a perfect defense. He was trying to keep a slightly deranged mother in good spirits.

Margali's letters to him were nowhere to be found; he must have destroyed them as soon as they'd been answered.

There was nothing else there more incriminating than about half a kilo of marijuana and a fair supply of cocaine. These items were evidence of a sort, but certainly not evidence of murder. I knew something like that had to be there; he never thought I'd spot the pen, so he had to be hiding some other kind of contraband.

The cocaine was rolled up in a plastic bag stuffed inside the toe of a boot, under two dirty socks.

The marijuana was in a blue school-type backpack on his closet shelf, with several dirty undershirts and jockey shorts lying on top of it.

Once or twice in my life, I'd seen better hiding places.

There wasn't anything else there that could be of any use to me. I returned to the den.

Bob Campbell was still searching for the will. I gathered that if it didn't turn up, they'd have to say Margali had died intestate, and that would make a lot of trouble for everybody. But Bob was searching alone now. Sam Lang, looking nearer eighty-five than seventy-five, was sitting on Margali's chaise longue. The blue veins were standing out on the backs of his hands.

"I noticed you took my whiskey," he said to me.

"Yes, sir, I did. I left a receipt for it on your desk."

"Why did you take my whiskey?"

"I left you four bottles."

"You took one and a half bottles. Why?"

"I thought it was a good idea."

"Was my wife trying to kill me? Was Marjorie trying to kill me? Or was it Jimmy? Was it my son? Did he want to kill me too?"

"I don't know." I really didn't. I hadn't gotten that far yet.

I knew Margali had originally—lightly—poisoned the soda pop cans herself. She'd made that clear. Oh, I couldn't have proved it in court, but I knew.

I knew she had to have help, because she hadn't bought—or even thought of—the soldering iron herself.

But Sam . . . who had tried to kill Sam? Margali, because he wouldn't let her drive, tried to control her drinking, tried to get her under the care of a psychiatrist? Or Jimmy, because . . .

Because if that will Margali had threatened him with wasn't lost—if it ever got back to Sam—then Sam had to die. Fast. Before Sam could read Margali's statement that Jimmy wasn't his son as he'd always believed, before Sam could change his will to disinherit a trouble-maker who was no kin to him.

Remembering Jimmy's expression when I mentioned that extra will, I knew whose hand had put the poison in Sam's whiskey. But whose was the original blame?

I would never know the answer to that one.

And I wouldn't tell Sam. Not until I had to.

So I contented myself with answering his original question as evasively as I could.

"I really don't know, Sam. I just—I just thought we'd better be safe."

"Safe?" He stared at me incredulously. "Safe? Sure—safe—without Marjorie, without Jimmy, without anything at all—you call that safe? What for? If you think—if you really think—my whiskey had anything in it that didn't belong in it, why didn't you just leave it for me to drink?"

"I can't do that, Sam."

"Why can't you? I left the cyanide for Lew to drink, real easy."

"That's—" I started to say, "That's you, not me." But I couldn't say it. I substituted, lamely, "That's not a thing I can do."

"I don't know how I could do it, either," Sam said. "But that was a long, long time ago, and besides, the wench is dead."

"Is that quite how the line goes?" I asked automatically.

"No. Not quite. But—it'll do. For now, it'll do." He was silent for a moment. Then, slowly, he added, "I used to go to plays. A long, long time ago—when Marjorie was alive—I used to go to plays."

I didn't know what to say to Sam Lang. There wasn't anything left. Even pity was cruel now. So I said briskly, "I've got another couple of ideas on where Margali's will might be, and I'm going to go check them out. I'll be back later."

I returned to my office first, to make not my formal report, which was going to take a long time, but an informal one, to Captain Millner, because the reporters had seen Jimmy leave in handcuffs, and the minute Millner stuck his nose outside his own office, the press'd be all over him like flies on shit. As they were on me, when I left the Lang house, when I entered the police station.

After telling Millner what was going on, I went down to the evidence vault and asked the clerk on duty to let me see Margali's purse for myself.

Everything was properly labeled, tagged, identified. I had to sign the chain-of-custody tag before I could even look at it, although I made it plain I wanted to look at it right there.

I wasn't interested in cosmetics, cologne, cash, a dainty

ladylike silver-chased pocket flask. I was interested in just one thing. A brown manila envelope.

Because Saturday, in the bookstore beside the Blue Owl, Margali had her purse open. I was beside her when she opened it. And I saw inside of it the bulging brown envelope, and inside that was the blue binding of the outside of a legal document—a wet blue binding.

The envelope was still there, but it wasn't bulging; there was no blue document in it. But the envelope—especially the inside—was water-stained.

She had her will with her before she went into the Blue Owl. She didn't have it when her body was found.

Our techs, searching the theater thoroughly, hadn't found it.

Which could mean that Jimmy had taken it out of her bag, or it meant the will was still in the theater. If he'd flushed it down the toilet, it would have stopped up the toilet. If he'd burned it, we'd have noticed the smoke, except that it was probably too wet to burn anyway. He couldn't have taken it out during the movie; the door was locked. He couldn't have taken it out after the movie, because he was searched.

So it had to be inside the building somewhere, and I intended to find it.

In the end it was ridiculously easy to locate. I didn't find it by being smart, by thinking where I would have hidden it if I were Margali. I found it by needing to go to the bathroom.

You know that kind of acoustic tile where they hang a sort of metal framework and then they set the tiles in the framework? Well, that's what they have in the rest rooms of the Blue Owl. And one of the tiles, in the women's rest room, was out of whack—just a little, as if it had been lifted out of its track and not set back in quite right. And if I looked from the right angle, I could see just a glimpse of water-spotted blue paper in behind it.

Margali wasn't much taller than I am. So she had to have,

gotten to it the same way I did, which was, closing the lid on the toilet and climbing on top of it and stretching as high as I could.

As my husband said later, yelling at me about it, Margali Bowman wasn't pregnant. But then on the other hand, Margali was a lot older than I, as I replied.

Anyway, I did get it down and I didn't fall, so what did Captain Millner want to yell at me about it for? And Dutch Van Flagg?

I am not a piece of blown glass or tissue paper.

The first thing I found was a beautiful emerald bracelet, three strings of square-cut emeralds on a gleaming gold setting. I estimated its worth as somewhat greater than that of my entire house, and I'd seen it on Margali many times. That alone told me I'd found that special hiding place she'd tried to tell me about.

Anybody but Margali would have realized that the electricians for the building would have found it in an instant, if they'd ever had to work on the wiring.

Beside the bracelet was one of those little velvet pouches of unset gems, appearing just like those Fara had showed me. The bracelet and gem pouch were loose, just sitting on the nearest square of acoustic tile. And behind them was a mass of folded paper. A will. A slightly damp will, signed "Marjorie Gorman Lang," still folded and creased just the way I had folded it to return it to Margali when the storm came up.

I didn't stop to read it.

When I got to my office again, there was—the secretaries told me—someone waiting to see me. A Jerry Alsford. They'd put him in a conference room to wait. No, they didn't know what Jerry Alsford wanted. He just wanted to talk to the detective handling the Margali Bowman killing. And he wouldn't talk to anyone else.

We get nuts that way, a lot of them. He might be going to

inform me that a team of Venusians with ray guns killed Margali Bowman. But on the other hand, we get a lot of help that way too. That was how Susan first came to see me; she wanted to talk with the detective on the Baker case.

But I still approached the conference room a little warily.

In most businesses, a conference room has a lot of nice tables and chairs. There are pictures on the wall, and bright no-glare lighting, and maybe a coffeepot.

In police work, a conference room is what we called an interview room when a janitor was a custodian, and an interrogation room when a janitor was a janitor. Now that the janitor is a sanitation engineer, the interrogation room is a conference room. But the sanitation engineer still empties the trash and scrubs the floor, and the conference room still contains a heavy table bolted to the floor so it can't be thrown, two or three uncomfortable chairs, and often an old filing cabinet or two stuck in there to get them out of the way.

Jerry Alsford was sitting politely upright on one of the chairs, hands folded on the briefcase in front of him—a briefcase that might hold anything from his lunch to a dismantled Uzi submachine gun.

Don't laugh. I saw a Uzi for sale at the flea market in Grand Prairie last time I was there. The dealer, whose federal firearms license was properly displayed on the wall of his little booth, assured me it 'had been properly disabled. I told him it might take all of thirty minutes to undisable it.

"Really?" he said with wide-eyed innocence. "Now, I didn't know that."

But Jerry Alsford rose with old-fashioned courtesy as I entered the room and said, "Good morning, Ms.—uh—Mrs. Ralston. I hope they didn't call you in from something important."

Equally politely, I urged him to be seated, sat down myself, and said I hoped he hadn't been waiting long. (About an hour, the secretaries had said, all wildly curious.)

"Oh, no, not at all, not at all." Despite the old-world manners, he had an unmistakably West Texas twang in his voice, and he looked to be no more than thirty. But it was a timeless thirty; his badly shaven neck was turkey-red inside a starched white cotton shirt, his dark suit looked off the rack at a discount store, and his tie was a little too wide and not quite the right color.

All of which meant that in another five or ten years he'd be a knockout as a trial lawyer, pulling that "just us folks" routine that juries love so much to a fare-thee-well. I'd have to remember Jerry Alsford.

His law firm was Alsford, Webster, and Alsford. Not quite Abbot, I thought, remembering the discussion between Sam and Bob, but close enough.

Mr. Jerry Alsford had an interesting story to tell, but first he wanted to make sure that Marjorie Gorman Lang was Margali Bowman. I assured him she was and offered to show him her birth certificate, but he said that wasn't necessary; under the circumstances my word was quite sufficient.

I assured him again that Marjorie Gorman Lang was Margali Bowman, and he said, "Then I've got something I think is going to interest you." He opened his briefcase and fussed around inside it, on the table, as I waited not very patiently. "She came to me last March, with this."

It was yet another will. The one Bob Campbell had made out, the one that was missing completely? Most likely.

"She said her husband and her lawyer were very close friends. She had to have a new will, but she didn't want her husband to know what was in it and she was afraid her lawyer would tell him. I assured her that was extremely unlikely, as it would be considered quite unethical, and she said— Well, she didn't think highly of lawyers' ethics." I tried not to laugh as he went on. "She told me she had let her attorney draw up a will for her, and she signed it. That was the will she turned over to me."

"All right," I said, and checked the date on it. March fourteenth. The one now in my briefcase was dated March seventeenth. I hadn't read it, but I had checked the date.

"And then she did a really peculiar thing. She had me draw up a new will for her according to extremely careful instructions. It contained some—ah—somewhat objectionable clauses, and she was clearly somewhat intoxicated, but she was—ah—quite clear on what she wanted; in fact, she wrote it all out herself on a yellow pad; and I had no real grounds for questioning her competence. She came back on March seventeenth to sign it."

"That doesn't sound terribly peculiar to me," I said.

"Oh, that's not what was peculiar. She came back on March seventeenth and duly signed the will and put it in her purse."

"Is this it?" I set the water-damaged document on the table.

"That's it," he said, after examining it carefully. "The two witnesses who signed are my secretary and my law clerk. As I said, she signed it and put in her purse. She asked for my bill—she'd told me she didn't want anything mailed to the house—and then she wrote me a check and handed it to me. And then, quite coolly, she told me she wanted me to draw up another will."

"What?" I said.

"That was what I said. And then she told me that in the will she had just signed she had made certain statements that were—ah—untrue. She said she wanted that will to—ah—'scare somebody with.' I believe those were her words. And now she wanted me to draw up her real will. I told her that under the circumstances—"

"What circumstances?"

"The circumstances she had just explained to me. I told her that under those circumstances I refused to draw up another will until she had given my secretary a signed, sworn statement detailing what she had just told me. She agreed to do that; we spent the next hour on the statement; and then I drew up her real will, which to my surprise contained exactly the same provisions as the will she had brought me to start with. It's quite ordinary—her husband, son, and daughter to be joint heirs; her husband and her attorney, Mr. Robert Campbell of Campbell, Blair, and Whatley, to be executors. Here is that will; she had requested that I watch the obituary column and turn the will over at the appropriate time to either Mr. Campbell or the police, at my discretion, depending on the manner of her death. It's dated March twentieth," he added, "and here's the statement I had her sign."

Margali's wild hares of ideas fairly leapt off the page; Alsford might have prompted with questions, but the secretary had typed Margali's own words.

In my will dated March seventeenth I stated that my son James Randolph Messick was conceived at a party and I did not know who his father was, but I had convinced my then husband Sunny Messick—that is Garner Moody Messick, the race driver—that it was his, conceived after our reconciliation, but after Sunny got killed on the racetrack I then convinced Samuel Clemens Lang, who is now my husband, that the baby was his, conceived before Sunny and I were reconciled. All of that is untrue. Or at least most of it is. What is true is that my son James Randolph Messick is the natural son of my present husband Samuel Clemens Lang. I am absolutely certain of that. There is no other possibility. I think Sunny did think it was his but I didn't tell him so. I just didn't tell him it wasn't, but he got killed anyway.

The reason I said that was to scare Jimmy. Jimmy is my son James Randolph Messick. Jimmy has some real good friends who are involved with the big movie studios that are producing now over in Las Colinas sort of between Dallas and Fort Worth and Jimmy could get them to get me a new movie or television show but he won't. Right now Jimmy is Sam's heir—that's my husband Samuel Clemens Lang—after me, but if Sam thought Jimmy wasn't his son then Sam wouldn't leave anything to him. So if Jimmy thinks I'll tell Sam then he'll get scared and he'll get me a good role.

But of course I wouldn't really tell Sam that because it isn't even true and besides that it would be mean. I don't care if I'm mean to Jimmy because he's mean and hateful to me and boys shouldn't be mean to their mothers, but I'd never do anything to hurt Sam because Sam's the only person who's always been nice to me.

It was signed Marjorie Gorman Lang, a.k.a. Margali Bowman.

"I told her that was extremely unwise," Alsford said. "I went farther, in fact. I told her that's the kind of behavior that gets people killed."

"It's certainly what got her killed," I agreed, refolding the statement. For the first time I was even sorry for Jimmy. She'd thrown a mentally unbalanced man a lot farther off balance, and simultaneously demanded the impossible from him.

"Let's you and me go call Bob Campbell," I added.

Before it was over we'd turned up six more lawyers who'd written wills for Margali. Not that it mattered anymore. As best we could determine, the water-damaged one was the last one.

Jimmy had remembered to get his fingerprints off the hypodermic syringe, the soldering iron, the Coke case. But the receipt for the soldering iron was in his room. I found it, the second time I searched, stuffed far back in a dresser drawer.

He'd wiped his fingerprints off the whiskey bottle. But you don't use fingerprint powder to raise fingerprints on paper. And you can't wipe fingerprints off paper, because they're not on the paper at all, they're soaked into the paper. The paper ring around the back of the whiskey bottle was the last nail in his coffin. A spray of ninhydrin—a shot of hot steam—and there they were, as pretty as you please, the prints of his left thumb and forefinger and his right forefinger.

So after all my theorizing, we finally had facts. It wasn't Margali, who'd semipoisoned herself and me, who'd tried to poison

Sam; it was Jimmy—it was Jimmy, pushed beyond endurance by threats he couldn't face and demands he couldn't meet. And it was Jimmy who'd killed Margali, hoping—perhaps believing, perhaps making himself believe because he wanted to believe it—that the will she'd held as a club over his head would never be found.

Probably it was Margali who killed Ali Hassan, but it could have been Sam. Probably it was Lew Mosier who killed Sunny Messick. Probably it was Sam Lang who killed Lew Mosier, although it might have been Margali. But all that was a long, long time ago and besides, the wench is dead . . . as Sam put it.

I don't know where Sam Lang is. He didn't want to stay around for the trial. He told us we were welcome to subpoena him if we thought we could find him. But we aren't going to try very hard. Why bother?

I think he's in Mexico, fishing; at least that's where Bob Campbell went, as soon as the trial date was tentatively set. He said he'd come back for the trial.

Fara and Edward are holding a revival in Marshall right now. I don't know whether I'll see Fara anymore. I tried to visit them, once, but Edward told me something about "sow the wind and reap the whirlwind," and Fara only cried, so I decided I'd better leave.

I don't think Edward Johnson and I worship the same God. After all, it wasn't Fara who sowed the wind. But she's sure doing the reaping.

Captain Millner was planning schedules the other day. He asked me when he ought to mark me off. I told him unless the doctor tells me otherwise, I'd probably need to take off about the middle or end of April.

He asked me when I'd be back. I told him I didn't know. After all, I never had a baby before.

Oh, and K-Mart sent me a refund and a nice little note of apology.

I'd forgotten all about that four-pack of toilet paper I didn't get home with. I was busy meditating on a very important decision I'd recently made.

I'll never, ever forget or change it.

It's this: I'm never going to go to another house party.